GLIMMER

In a world where

light and darkness

are equal, which one

would you choose?

ELLE JAINES

For everyone who thinks they can't…you can.

#DREAMBIGWORKHARD

PROLOGUE

Racing through the dense undergrowth, her feet swollen from thorns, Dawn hid precariously behind the jagged tree stump, her heart beating in her throat, pulsating erratically at the chase. He knew she loved the thrill, she always had. That is how it all started, a dangerous game of cat and mouse, two forbidden souls entangled in a tragic tale. It is how all the best stories started, Dawn rationalised in her head every time they had to say goodbye, conveniently leaving out the fated endings.

It was getting dark, the sun was setting around them, she would have to leave soon to avoid getting caught. Peeping around the edge of the haggard tree she listened for crackles in the grass, she should be able to feel his approach by now but his deceit obscured her senses. She had to be home by nightfall, that was the rule.

'Okay, I give up' shouted a voice from beyond the trees. Dawn remained hidden, she had a few minutes till sunset and she couldn't let him win.

'You're the one with the curfew, I can be out all night if I want' he continued.

The voice was louder this time, closing in on its prey. Dawn let the final moments of daylight wash over her, she wished it could be like this forever, her dizzy teenage dream transforming into reality, but it would never be, not for them. She already knew that. His cool hands cupped her waist from behind,

'Found you', a rush of shivers pulsed through her body, their magnetism drawing them together on a physical and spiritual level.

'I've got to go' said Dawn pulling his hands away, she meant every word but was absorbed by him.

'I'll walk you home' he said, his gesture sweet but too dangerous.

'No, its fine, I'll go from here, it's only four blocks and we don't want to draw in any unwanted attention. I wish it didn't have to be like this...' said Dawn.

'It doesn't, we can make it together you and me, we can abandon this whole life and just be us' he replied.

Dawn admired his optimism, she let the thought cleanse her soul, picturing the life they could have together, but it meant both of them making the ultimate sacrifice.

'Don't do it Dawn, they can't make you, I can't even think about you being with him, don't do it, for me...' he begged

'I have no choice; you know that. It's not like that anyway, we're not getting married'

He pulled away from her putting distance between them, hurt by her final words. Dawn turned to make her way home, guilt and sadness echoing in her feeble steps. This was not what she wanted, but it had to happen.

'Dawn' he said

She paused, still facing away from him

'You will always be mine Dawn'

Her heart fluttered in response, a torrent of ripples radiating through her body, fear and love combined into one statement. Her seventeen-year-old self, writing off the commanding nature of his declaration. She did not turn around again but knew his eyes followed her every movement. As she walked away, she whispered under her breath,

'...and   you   will   be   mine   Devin'

CHAPTER 1

RAEGAN

It was raining that night; she could hear the small patterned taps on the windowpane. It was hard to stay asleep when it rained, her broken sleep plagued by countless nightmares dancing playfully in her head. The dreams had grown worse in recent nights, the level of realism terrified Raegan, so much so it was hard to distinguish what was real and what was not. The content had also changed, she dreamt of people she had never met, strangers regularly trespassing her subconscious, their pain nestling deep into her spirit to find solace. The visuals changed every night, she rarely saw the same image more than once, tonight was the same, her head bursting with tortured fantasies, an utter contradiction of her normal teenage life. Raegan knew this pain, she had felt it, not just through others but truly felt it. It was still raining when she finally admitted defeat, opening her misty blue eyes and staring she begrudgingly at her cell phone; 4.04am. Only one hour and fifty-six minutes until her alarm would attempt to rouse her with its serene gong and water sounds. The darkness didn't scare her, it felt cool and soothing, it had a peaceful quality to it, it allowed her to think, something that Raegan often avoided. Thinking was dangerous, thinking scared her. She squinted again at her cell phone, 4.08am; this was going to be a long day.

Raegan dragged her limbs from the warmth of her bed and turned on the bathroom light, the beam hit her eyes like a thousand high resolution pixels, she slammed them shut for a second then slowly released staring directly into her reflection. She scanned her face, her burnt orange hair falling ungracefully over her temple, her milky white complexion stained by the dregs of yesterday's mascara; for seventeen she looked mature. Her eyes could tell a million stories, not just her own but those of others. She stared deep into her reflection and was greeted by an abundance of vivid memories, it had always been like this, for as long as she could remember. A few years earlier, a week before her eighth birthday she had met a strange lady with murky eyes on the bus home from school, the woman did not utter a single word to her but Raegan knew her spirit, could sense her fears, ambitions, lies, she felt it all. The dreams had started soon after the fateful meeting and had become a regular part of her life. Her nightmares made it difficult to decipher dreams from reality, what was truly hers and what was not, she was in a constant state of disorientation, the limbo haunted her. She kept her distance from most people, choosing carefully who to communicate and interact with, friendship didn't often come into it. Being seventeen was hard enough, the last thing

Raegan needed was to be cast further outside the realm of normality by subtlety mentioning her 'issues'.

One person she had let into her life was Alice. Raegan and Alice had been best friends since junior school, she wasn't one hundred percent sure how their friendship had developed but she knew she could not survive high school without her. Alice was a free spirit, carefree; floating from place to place on the journey she called *life*. Raegan looked in awe at Alice and wondered how she got here. Both her mother and father were nothing like her, the exact opposite in fact, her mother was a PA to a company director for a big important law firm and her father works in the movie business. Both worked more than they played in stressful and intense environments; how two people can come together to make another person so different to themselves baffled Raegan. Surely there are genetic measures in place to avoid this, although she was no expert, and her parents were not perfect test subjects themselves. Raegan never really knew her mother, but she was sure she could not be so different to herself. She had seen cheerful photographs and heard amusing stories, but of all the memories she had inside her head not one of them was of her mother, not her smile, her smell or even her laugh, nothing. She was just an empty space, like a canvas that had been hung but never touched by paint. Raegan took in a long cleansing breath to rid her body of all feeling, exhaling the demons that tormented her. The buzzing of the light rang through her ear drum causing an uncomfortable ache in the base of her neck. Her palms started to feel damp with sweat, Raegan knew this feeling and she recognised what was coming, her breath drew shallow as she gripped the side of the cold basin. It was the heat that was the worst, an inner combustion took over her senses, the heat travelled through her veins into every crease and crinkle; she imagined her blood thick like lava, bubbling through her body, melting her organs one by one. The heat continued for a few long seconds then as quick as it started, it left. Raegan collapsed into a puddle on the floor, her bed shirt soaked through. She stared up at the bathroom light willing it to go off so she could rest for a while, but it did not, it stubbornly glared at her, but she was finished. She closed her eyes and drifted off to sleep on the cold damp tiles.

6am came quickly, the ritual predictability of the alarm; Raegan could hear the mellow tones and water droplets echoing from her cell phone. Her body was heavy like the aftermath of a spin class she once attended. Piece by piece she picked herself off of the cool floor and turned off the alarm, she could already smell her Dads coffee seeping through the hallways. It was a comforting smell, a reassuring *'everything is ok'* smell, and reassurance is something Raegan needed in her life at the moment.

'Morning precious' was another of her dads reassuring traits and something that she expected to hear every morning.

'You sleep ok? I heard some commotion in the early hours, not getting in from a late night rave were you?' he said in jest,

'Yeah Dad, that's exactly it'.

Raegan was aware that sarcasm was the lowest form of wit, but it worked for her. She could see the steam rising from her Dad's coffee and it sent a shiver through her spine,

'You ok Rae? you look at little peaky' he said moving close to her face and cupping her cheeks carefully in both hands. He moved her head side to side looking deeply into her eyes, as if he were searching for an answer to a question he hadn't verbalised. She could smell his hand cream occupying her nostrils, it had a light rustic twist to it, not too feminine to put his single status into question. Raegan didn't know many men, but she was sure that her dad's obsession with his hands wasn't normal.

'I'm fine dad, just had a rough night' she said grabbing a slice of cold, limp toast from the plate and moving swiftly out of the front door

'Got to dash' she said, slamming the door behind her, her body drenched with relief at her hasty exit, she didn't want to fend off too many questions, especially ones she could not yet answer.

Chapter 2

RAEGAN

The journey to school was never eventful; Raegan had lived in the same town most of her life so she could trace her steps to school with both eyes shut, walking backwards. Today was like any other day, a light breeze in the spring air, the potent smell of motor oil pouring out of Mr McKenzie's car garage swiftly drowned out by the sweet warmth of Franco's Italian bakery. Raegan could already feel the clement sun press on the back of her neck; she pulled her collar up to cover her skin from the harsh rays and walked quickly to the corner of the street.

'What is wrong with me' she scolded to herself, resting her head back on the cool brick wall. In her peripheral vision she could see a young woman, mid-twenties, walking sharply towards her, Raegan's eyes moved carefully scanning the woman from bottom to top eventually making direct eye contact. That was a mistake, everything was happening in slow motion, the young women's eyes were hazel brown and were filled with sadness, Raegan could feel the sadness, a lost hope, a barren land of missed opportunities. She held the woman's gaze witnessing a flicker of memory or thought pattern, the searing pain that had encapsulated her only hours before was creeping back inside her body. She needed to stop it; this couldn't happen here, she needed to control it. With all of her strength Raegan broke eye contact with the woman and she continued on her way past as if nothing had happened. She took a deep breath and pulled herself together, beads of sweat pooled in the palms of her hands, her heart still throbbing with a drum and bass rhythmic quality.

'Are you ok?' said a voice from the shadows,

'Hey, you ok? it repeated,

Raegan took a deep soothing breath and squinted through the sun, walking towards her was a tall figure wearing blue chinos and sneakers. Raegan's full vision hadn't returned yet, but the concerned stranger appeared to be shrouded in shade, managing to focus again she stood up straight.

'Yes, I'm fine, just a little lightheaded, must be the heat' she said

'Right…' he paused unconvinced by her alibi, 'Although it's not actually that hot today'.

Raegan was about to come back with a witty comment when she caught the shaded figures eye, her breath trapped by two crystal blue cyclones swallowing up her ingenious comment. She had lost her words, there was no pain in his eyes or happiness or feeling at all, he was emotionally mute.

'Yes, thank you. I'm fine; I just need to get going' said Raegan breaking her gaze.

'Wait, wait', two seconds ago you were barely vertical now you want to just run away', he had an assured confidence in his voice that preceded his arrogance.

'Again, I'm fine, thank you, just need to get to school' she said edging further away from him,

'School, which school?' his voice inquisitive to her revelation.

'Shaylock High, just three blocks from here' she said hoping to end the conversation there.

'Ah, me too, I'll walk with you'.

Raegan needed to get away, as much he intrigued her, his hollowness made her fearful, she couldn't grasp the feeling, but it felt uncontrollable. A basic human fight or flight reflex overcame her, adrenaline pulsing through her veins making her legs twitch, she needed to go.

'Ah, great, well I'll see you there, I've got some errands to run first, thanks for the offer' and she scurried away down the street.

'At least tell me your name', said the obscure stranger his voice drifting down the alley. Raegan sensed she shouldn't, but the words left her lips in an involuntary motion.

'Raegan Cole'

'Well nice to meet you Raegan, if we meet again you can call me Dom'. She barely made out the second part of his name as her scurry turned into a sprint, but the first part was etching its way into her brain, letter by letter the way a hot poker melts and scars you for life.

*   *   *   *

Raegan landed on Alice's doorstep a shaky, scrambling mess; she grasped the large brass doorknocker and slammed it against the door. Alice was never ready for school, her free-spirited nature didn't allow for it, it was impossible for her to maintain sociably acceptable time keeping. Raegan had called in for Alice every day for the last eight years and every day she was running late. She had developed several strategies to combat her tardiness including being early and late herself, but nothing had worked. Alice's parents worked long hours so were seldom home to encourage their daughter to participate in time keeping. The large door opened to reveal a short, brown haired girl standing in the hallway wearing a knee length floral skirt, a slip knot mini tee and brown retro Doc Martin boots.

'Ready to go?' said Raegan hopefully,

'Yep, just two secs' and she raced off in the opposite direction. Raegan often wondered whether it was Alice's free-spirited nature that made her dress this way or if it was more of a dig at her conventional parents and their conventional lives.

'Geez, what happened to you this morning? You look like hell!' said Alice sniggering under her breath. As well as making its way out through her clothes her free spirit also had a free mouth and wasn't afraid to say what she thought.

'Thanks, it's just been a bit hectic this morning that's all' Raegan replied,

'What more psychic Sally stuff' she said in gest.

'Keep it down, I don't want the worlds weirdest weirdo's channel banging on my door'. Raegan walked out of the house closely followed by Alice.

'Alarm set, double bolted, check, the house resembling Fort Knox, check' Alice shared Raegan's love of sarcasm, it was probably one of the reasons they got on so well.

'So, what's up Rae?' her compulsion to know the drama assisting their journey to school.

'Not much, I don't really…' Raegan was interrupted mid-sentence by her cell phone, she dug into her jacket pocket and looked at the screen.

'It's my Gran, damn it', she swiped her finger promptly across to cancel the call.

'What's that about? asked Alice, 'Your Gran rocks',

'Yeah she does, but I can't deal with her right now, she keeps wanting to talk about serious things'. Raegan stared at the message alert that popped up on the screen and for a second, she felt a shred of guilt about brushing her off,

'I just can't deal with her right this minute, I'll call her later, it'll be fine'.

'So, Rae, you haven't filled in the blanks, what happened last night?' Raegan didn't want to share too many details in case it frightened even Alice.

'Nothing big, just woke up, felt dizzy, then crashed again' crashed being an understatement.

Raegan's reaction to talking about emotion was not uncommon, she did not deal well with it and Alice did not push her. They had met at a pivotal point in Raegan's life, she was weak, vulnerable and a shadow of a child, the trauma that had gone through at such a young age was just too much. Alice never discovered the full extent of the Raegan's mother's disappearance, she wasn't even sure if Raegan had unearthed the whole truth, her memories of the matter were broken and fragmented, none of them complete. Raegan had lived with her Dad ever since and whilst they were happy together the void left from her Mother's disappearance was ever present. It went quiet, a moment of contemplation for both girls before they entered the abyss masked as education.

The streets were alive in the morning, children were packing into well-kept cars, men dressed in immaculate white shirts and women walking in heels that Raegan could only imagine wearing. She always tried to avoid the busyness, it was too risky especially if she had one of her episodes around lots of people, she was unstable at the moment and it worried her. Alice didn't share her view, she had made a game out of her 'issue',

'Tell me Rae' Alice pleaded doe-eyed 'please',

'If I lose it, it's on your head' said Raegan with a smirk in her voice.

Usually, Raegan kept her head down whilst walking through crowds, looking directly in front of her avoiding eye contact at all costs but for this game she had to break this rule. Alice's name for her was 'psychic Sal' because of her natural intuition, she could sense people's emotions and feelings then make up stories about them, but what Alice didn't realise was that she was not making up the stories, she was streaming them, For her it was a mindless game to pass time on the way to school, for Raegan a game of Russian roulette with the odds placed out of her favour.

'Her, over there in the red shoes', said Alice excitedly, Raegan glanced up momentarily,

'She's anxious, has a new job, fancies her new boss'

Alice giggled.

'Tell me more'.

Raegan continued the tall tale about the stranger in the red shoes, how she brought her Versace bag on layaway and how her dog yapped at any new man she brought back to her cramped studio apartment. To Alice it was like an episode of a soap opera, filling in the juicy details of someone else's life, but Raegan saw much more in the red shoes, a vulnerability, a fear of the boss she was about to meet and a sense of isolation in her lonely apartment. This was the part she didn't share.

'Ok, again, again', Alice begged 'that guy standing on the corner in the black jacket'

Raegan lifted her eye line to get a glimpse of the stranger but before he could fully fill her vision, her heart started racing, she could sense the danger in the air, the dark shadow that surrounded him made her restless. Time slowed; her vision reduced to a blur as she caught her breath. He was staring directly back at her.

'Come on, what do you think?... my future husband? Alice's humour broke the connection,

'I can't think Alice, I can't read anything from him' she snapped back, which wasn't a total lie.

'Come on or we won't just be late, we'll be detention late'.

Raegan ushered Alice quickly around the corner past the sinister stranger. You could hear the buzz of the school before you could see it, it had a similar sound to a hive with hundreds of students buzzing in and out of the building. They turned the corner of 51st street and looked apprehensively at the grand building. It looked no different to most high schools in suburban America; it had a majestic frontage, tall off-white columns standing either side of the entrance with a set of polished windows sat side by side above the door. The buzz of students was starting to quieten as Alice and Raegan dashed into the hallway. Raegan was not a fan of running; in fact, the only running she ever did voluntarily was running to class.

'See you in Bio' said Alice under her breath as she entered her Math class. Raegan continued quickly down the long hall desperately hoping that Mr Griggs was running late too. Mr Griggs was one of the most feared members of the faculty at Shaylock High, he was strict, unforgiving and took pleasure in ritualistic humiliation. Raegan cautiously peaked into the classroom through the small window to get a flavour of the humiliation that awaited her,

'Dare I ask?' a recognisable voice whispered from behind. Raegan didn't need to turn around to know who it was,

'We must stop meeting like this' said Dom, the words teasing from his mouth.

'Shhhhh' Raegan signalled pressing her index finger sternly against her mouth. Dom moved next to her to see inside the classroom, the room was silent, not a peep of noise, heads were down looking at the thick textbooks that were a constant reminder of the monumental task at hand. Mr Griggs was nowhere to be seen, an invisible presence in the room. Raegan glanced to the side, Dom was gone, she whipped her head around to see him standing calmly next to the lockers, his arrogance was the first thing that she could sense, beyond that he was a black hole. She shook her head and looked back through the small window to be greeted by two wrinkled brown eyes looking displeased at the situation on the other side of the door.

'Miss Cole, Mr Carter, were you planning on joining us today or just spectating?', Raegan's cheeks flushed with embarrassment.

'Sorry Sir' she said placing her hand on the door frame to enter the room. Stepping forward Dom's hand mirrored hers, the moment was brief but electrifying, a chemical combustion that embraced her entire being, she felt agony and numbness all at the same time, a mixture of bright lights and obscure darkness. A rush of fragmented images pierced Raegan's mind, a fusion of bright shapes and colours layered like a broken kaleidoscope. Although she couldn't make out what the images were, there was a strange sense of familiarity to them, like she had seen them before. The moment stopped as quickly as it started. Mr Griggs stood impatiently in the doorway waiting for the two students to enter.

'In your own time' he barked.

Twenty-two bodies turned to stare, the room fell silent, but Raegan could hear the barrage of backstabbing aimed her way. Raegan took her seat, three rows in front of Dom. The rest of the lesson was a blur, her head felt fuzzy; a layer of fog shrouded her thoughts like a scene from a 1920's silent horror movie. In her world they were only two people in the room, an intense spotlight focused on them. Mr Griggs was talking about symbolism in sonnets but Raegan couldn't hear him clearly, his voice was muffled by two crystal blue eyes penetrating her peripheral vision. She knew he was looking but she couldn't bring herself to meet his gaze. The temptation to look was torture; it took every muscle to control herself. Who was he? Why hadn't she noticed him before? Raegan kept glancing at the white clock above Mr Griggs desk willing it to speed up, every tick, every tock lasting an eternity. He didn't take his eyes off of her; she was convinced he hadn't blinked the entire time. As she sat replaying the previous morning in her head the school bell announced itself through a sharp and unsettling bleep, she jumped up and bustled out of the classroom pushing past anyone in her path. Running dramatically through the wide corridor she pushed open the bathroom door and threw herself into a cubicle. She started to overheat, her heart was beating in double time, her breath rapidly becoming too quick for her chest to cope.

'Come on Rae' she begged herself. After a few seconds she perched cautiously on the top of the toilet seat focussing on her breathing, she couldn't pass out, not here. Someone would find her, take a picture and share it with the world and that is all she needed. Slowly she began to feel normal again but contemplated spending the rest of the school day in the bathroom. After her rational sense of mind came back, she noticed the pungent bleach and soap odour that filled the room and finally decided to relocate.

CHAPTER 3

RAEGAN

'Where did you get to earlier? I was looking everywhere for you' said Alice slamming her heap of textbooks abruptly on the wooden desk.

'Shhhhh' came a voice from the corner of the room. The school library was vast for a suburban high school, the smell was unique, it seeped out of the walls surrounding the room seemingly to both protect it from unruly guests and inviting in others. The shelves were three stories high crammed with years and years of knowledge, fact and fiction. Raegan often pondered on how, if ever, you would get to those books, she had never seen a ladder or even anybody trying to reach for them, they were docile, stagnant, ancient in her eyes. Alice's sudden appearance had disrupted her sanctuary, she needed somewhere to think, and this was the perfect place, just her and her thoughts.

'Hey' Alice repeated, more forcefully this time, Raegan lifted her head from the desk showing some recognition of her arrival. Alice clambered around the other side of the desk hastily shoving her nose in a book to avoid detection from the librarian. Mrs Kane was a stickler for chatterboxes; her supersonic hearing could sense even a whisper. Raegan was sure the room was bugged; she looked under the desks several times for micro devices but nothing. Raegan reached over to Alice and turned the book the correct way up, smirking as she did it.

'I'm working Alice' she said semi-sternly,

'Remember the concept, teacher sets work, we do work, it's a give and take scenario', Alice could taste the sarcasm in Raegan's voice

'Ha ha' she replied.

'Why are you hiding all the way back here?' said Alice in her best whispering voice. Raegan had positioned herself in the oldest section of the library, no computers, iMacs, photocopying machines, it was a tiny retreat from the chaos of the world and that was the way she liked it.

'I'm trying to concentrate, we have a Math test in the morning' she lied, her mind couldn't concentrate on Math, after the encounter this morning she could barely string a sentence together. She didn't know why she wanted to be in the library, but it felt safe, the books comforted her, silent and shielding. As Raegan continued to scribble in her journal an icy silence covered the room, even the air was still. Only the loud creaking door cut through the tranquillity. It could have been one of a thousand students but instinctively Raegan grabbed her bag and pulled Alice into the aisle between the old books.

'Wait, what?' said Alice, Raegan pushed her finger forcefully to her lips. She positioned herself strategically so she could peep through the brown tinged back catalogues, after a couple of seconds Alice's eyes joined her.

'What are we looking at?' she said squinting her eyes in the same direction as Raegan,

'Shhhhh' Raegan responded focussing her eyes on the large polished door, she had barely blinked in the past minute, she wasn't sure what she was looking for, but she knew something was amiss. Raegan continued to look towards the door; something was pulling her gaze.

'How long are we going to wait like this Rae?'

Raegan turned to Alice to give her a comforting grin, as she turned back to the Grand entrance a dark figure sloped out of the door, she only caught the back of his head but she knew it was him.

'What are we even waiting for?' said Alice impatiently. Raegan wanted to answer her, she wanted to tell her everything, but she couldn't, not yet.

The lunchroom was its usual frenzy; Raegan and Alice sat on the wooden benches at the back of the cafeteria. Raegan sat quietly dissecting the sandwich her dad had made her; there wasn't a lot of variation in her household, especially when it came to lunch. Today's special was tuna, she picked the mottled crust off of the sides and broke the bread into small sections, placing them back in the reused brown paper bag,

'What happened Rae?' said Alice, her eyebrows pointing down in concern,

'Come on, I know something happened, you're never this quiet!'

Raegan sat ignorantly staring at her unappealing lunch.

'Right, well, I'm just gonna ask Conner then, he was in your English class' she said turning swiftly around packing up her lunch, obviously trying to call Raegan's bluff,

'Wait' slipped begrudgingly from Raegan's lips,

'I'll tell you, but not here'.

The girls packed up their things and quickly disappeared from the canteen.

'Where are we going?' said Alice,

'Just shhhh' Raegan replied pulling Alice's coat down the long corridor. They reached an old wooden door with D4 etched above it;

the room was desolate with little to no school equipment left. The floor was uneven where the cheap plastic tiles had lifted off of the concrete and there was a strong smell of damp that lingered in their nostrils.

'Jeez Rae, how do you know about this place? it's so cool', said Alice fascinated by the unknown space. Raegan shrugged; Alice didn't need to know the answer to that question. They clambered over the fallen tube lights, crushing small shards of glass underfoot; they stopped just short of the flaky rotting desk that sat still in the corner of the room. Alice didn't ask again; she knew that the more she pushed Raegan the further she would push her away. At least six minutes passed before Raegan uttered a word.

'I can't really explain it Alice, I don't really know myself' she said feeling exposed. Raegan sat with her head in her hands trying to articulate to Alice as best she could about her dreams, her attacks and most of all her brush with the estranged new boy, Dom. Alice sat motionless trying to make sense of all the information that had just overloaded her mind. Raegan stood up breaking the silence in the room and moved towards the old blackboard, she glanced at her cell phone, three missed calls from the same contact, before Alice could see she slipped the phone back into her bag.

'So, who is this Dom? Have we seen him before? asked Alice,

'I've never seen him before, but I am not the most perceptive person.'

'Have you told your Gran?'

'What do you think?', it's not the easiest subject to squeeze into a conversation'.

Raegan continued to tip toe around the room, making a game out of avoiding the shards of broken bulb that littered the floor.

'Well you can't just become a recluse because of one person Rae, you can't keep hiding like this' said Alice bluntly.

Raegan poised on one foot enjoying the glass crunch under her weight, out of the corner of her eye she caught a glint of something in the doorway, moving gingerly forwards she squinted her eyes to try and make sense of the obtuse shape. As she stepped closer the shape started to take form, his broad shoulders and scruffy hair unmistakable in silhouette form. For a moment she was lost in him, he swallowed her whole like a snake consuming its prey. She held his gaze for a few moments absorbing him, exploring his eyes for something, anything. Before she could call out to Alice, she fell to the floor, her feet collapsing beneath her as she slammed her slight body against the concrete. Her heartbeat began slow, each flutter feeling fainter than the last. She could hear shouting, probably Alice panicking, but she was paralysed, her body unresponsive to her own commands. Her last conscious vision was of him, skulking in the shadows, a smoky cloud drifting further and further from her grasp. Then   it   all   went   black.

CHAPTER 4

RAEGAN

Raegan wasn't quite sure what happened next, scattered pieces of the puzzle plagued her brain, flashing lights, a plastic mask covering her mouth, coffee breath and his eyes. When she woke, she wasn't in her bed, the sheets were stiffer against her skin and her head was lifted too high on the nylon pillows. The smell was recognisable, a gentle homeliness overcame her, a smell she had experienced many times before. Her Gran didn't live in a cottage or in a holiday village apartment; she lived on the third floor of a run-down estate building on the other side of town. The place was so old it didn't even have an elevator and the stone steps that led up to each floor crumpled unsteadily underfoot. Her Gran had struggled with the steps for years but was stubborn about moving, she had paid off the lease years ago, but Raegan suspected it was something more symbolic holding her there. She could barely pull herself to a sitting position, her body burdened by the dramatic fall. She looked around the room, it was plain, nothing fancy, no floral patterns or dowdy chairs, just a few silver photo frames cradling happy memories from days past. Raegan's eyes panned the photos one by one picking out small details; the taste of the ice cream that smothered her mouth as a child, the weightless floating feeling of descending on a swing. On the third picture she paused and shifted her legs from under the covers. Wobbling slightly on her feet she edged slowly towards a colour drained picture, a woman in her early twenties stared lovingly back at her, she should have recognised her, she wanted to recognise her. Her autumn brown hair fell full onto her shoulders, her simple lips and perfect teeth, Raegan couldn't see the resemblance herself, but others could.

'Beautiful, isn't she' said a voice intruding from the doorway, Raegan continued to stare at the image oblivious of her Grans presence.

'You look just like her… same dazzling eyes'.

Her Gran walked slowly to the bed and signalled Raegan to join her. Raegan moved into the designated space and perched uncomfortably shunning her Grans actions.

'Are you going to tell me what happened today or am I going to have to interrogate Alice? You know she wouldn't last ten seconds under my scrutiny'

Raegan hid her smile.

'Come on love, you can tell me anything' said her Gran. Raegan sat stubbornly avoiding contact, she knew if she caught her eye there would be no stopping the gush of emotion.

'Ok, shall I tell you a story instead,'

Her Gran shuffled onto the bed plumping the stiff cushions. Raegan reluctantly sat back, gazing down at her hands.

'Come on, just humour me, like old times… I once knew a girl about your age who was having some, let us call them 'troubles', she was a bright, beautiful young lady, driven to succeed and always surrounded by people. One day, these things started to change, just small changes at first, she couldn't concentrate at school, she started to feel isolated by those around her, she began to be plagued but headaches, dizzy spells, insomnia' Raegan's ears pricked up.

'Then she started having these blackouts, missing chunks of time, heart palpitations that would challenge a steam engine in a race. Doctors were baffled as every test they did came back with a normal result; she was a medical enigma. Every few days that past added more complications to her never ending list of ailments, her parents were so concerned as she was moving into her final year of high school and she was barely making it to two classes a day. Then, one day it all disappeared, every single symptom. But this girl had changed, none of us could pinpoint how, but she seemed tranquil, she had a spark about her that filled the room with hope', her Gran looked fondly into the distance as Raegan rudely interrupted her story,

'So, you're saying what Gran? She got better all by herself? A miracle? Wow that is a story, I think it's about six years too late for me though, I grew out of make-believe a while ago'.

'I didn't say it was make-believe did I, just a story. In this mood dear you are in no state to have a sensible discussion' she snapped.

'Sensible, you're here telling me stories about people who glow and have strength and then yelling at me for not being sensible!' said Raegan clearly irritated by the anecdote.

'I'll leave you dear' said her Gran walking sombrely out of the room.

Filling her lungs in frustration a weight of guilt slowly sunk in, she knew she shouldn't have spoken to her Gran like that; she was just trying to help in her own way. Raegan pulled the covers up over her head and closed her eyes tight wishing the ground beneath her would swallow her up, rest would help ease her pain, and time would hopefully ease her Grans.

*   *   *   *

Whether it was the guilt or not, the dreams were worse that night, it was as if everyone she had come in contact with that day had left an unconscious imprint on her. The dreams were fast, rushed and emotionally taxing, jumping from one person's torment with food to another person's sorrow for an early miscarriage. The feelings made her weary and sapped all her strength, she couldn't escape it and she felt utterly powerless. 6.05am, Raegan startled awake staring bleary eyed at the ceiling, she picked out some small brown tea stains to focus her vision. As her senses recovered from her restless night she was greeted by commotion and noise downstairs, a muffle of voices followed by a light tap on the door.

'Rae, Rae, are you awake?' said a familiar voice.

'Can I come in?',

Raegan sat up in the bed and pulled the covers over her lap, the door shuddered open and her Dad shuffled in placing himself awkwardly on the side of the bed,

'Hey' he said,

'Hey' replied Raegan bashfully,

'So, Gran tells me you have been having a bit of a tough time recently',

Raegan didn't reply, her closed stance saying everything.

'Do you want to talk about it?'

Another icy silence followed.

'Ok, well when you feel ready, I am here and so is Gran... I've brought your school things over, so I'll see you when you get in later'.

Raegan looked away rejecting his plight, he stood up and swiftly moved towards the door. Before he could leave he lingered for a moment at a space on the wall, something caught his eye, a small canny smile evaded the corner of his mouth as if he was remembering a private joke, as the moment past he left the room. Raegan had a million things running through her mind and school was not one she wanted to contemplate after yesterday's disaster. She would be all everyone talked about, side-lined glances and venomous whispers would haunt her all day, maybe all semester. How would she explain herself to Alice? What if he was there? How would she cope seeing him? The onslaught of questions that were rushing through her mind were acutely interrupted by her toe hitting the cold floor, she was going to school.

CHAPTER 5

RAEGAN

The journey to school was tedious, Raegan wasn't sure she was fully conscious; she imagined this was what it felt like to be exceedingly drunk, she had explored white rum with Alice at a sleepover once but she couldn't stomach the taste, it had made her light headed but it didn't last for more than an hour.

Raegan cruised through first and second period with the occasional head nod and scrappy note in her journal, she couldn't focus, she felt vulnerable just waiting for something to happen. She hadn't seen him today but she could sense him, they had a dangerous connection and Raegan could tell that it was going to escalate. She sat in the canteen stirring her milky coffee repeatedly watching the sandy brown liquid spiral inside the cup. Murmuring eyes gauged into her back, empty whispers filled the room silently interrogating her. The bemusement in their minds trying to decipher what had happened in that derelict room. Alice had obviously kept quiet but she was nowhere to be seen, her absence disturbed Raegan, she felt abandoned and estranged from the rest of her peer group. She needed to find her and explain what had happened, explain that it wasn't her fault, that she had done nothing wrong. She gulped the luke-warm coffee wincing at the bitter aftertaste, scuttling across the cafeteria in her usual clumsy fashion. As she moved through the crowd, noticing that the commotion had halted, muted eyes focused on the figure that had just entered the room. It was as if the crowded canteen had emptied and left just the two of them. Every move she made he counteracted like a game of human chess, his presence growing ever stronger in the room, asserting his dominance over the situation. To Raegan, the room was closing in, she began to suffocate, blood searing through her veins and beads of sweat collected on her brow. She felt like the world was watching but realistically no one had noticed a thing, in the frenzy of the cafeteria she was lost, stranded amongst a sea of half eaten trays and spilt soda. As the seconds ticked by her heart began beating in her throat, it was slowing much like the day before, she struggled to pull her heavy feet forward endeavouring to dodge Dom but eventually realising her escape was over. The hustle of the room overwhelmed her, all sound had been magnified to a deafening drone, she was unsure which sounds were real and which were just in her head. Her body began to shut down, but she felt thankful, a single tear formed in the corner of her eye, if this was to be it, then so be it. She descended to the coral coloured floor unaware that Dom was ready to catch her, as he grasped her limp body an explosion of light engulfed the room, a magnetic pulse threw Dom clear of their embrace. Both lay still on opposite sides of the room whilst hysteria filled the space, a torrent of teachers, medics and onlookers crowded Raegan looking for signs of life. On the other side of the room Dom's body lay contorted amongst plastic chairs and table legs, both were in critical conditions momentarily departed from their beings. Raegan's eyes fluttered delicately in the chaos, her hair resting carefully over her cheekbone as she breathed in a full tank of air; the inhale extended as her senses gradually returned. An unknown voice yelled close to her head; the vibrations of footsteps being directed away from the scene shuddered against her skin. A metallic tang lingered on her tongue; her lips felt dry to the touch but a moment later she opened her eyes wide to the world. Numbness subsided her as she hauled her body from the ground and stood tall amongst the crowd. To the naked eye she looked no different, but she could feel a warm glow surrounding her, a luminous energy that coated her from top to toe. Gasps echoed around the room as Raegan strolled out of the canteen unscathed. Several distressed faces mouthed gestures of concern, but Raegan was oblivious, she had her mind set on escaping the school, the town, the state, just getting away. In the cafeteria Dom lay still on the floor slowly gaining consciousness, as the minutes lapsed Raegan could feel him recovering but she knew she needed to stay away. Walking confidently away from the tall moth-eaten building questions were brewing.

'She knows... I know she knows...' Raegan repeated over and over.

The journey home was smooth and uneventful, Raegan glided through the bustling town, she felt untouchable. Her eyes fixed on the depleted building just meters in front of her, standing boldly at the entrance door she pressed the misshapen button.

'Gran, Gran' she called out impatiently,

'Gran, I need to talk now…Gran I know you're in there, please let me in'. Another resident of the building glanced out of her window peering suspiciously at Raegan,

'Gran' she repeated,

'Please'.

She stood pleading, waiting cautiously then finally admitting defeat leaning her head forward against the cold glass pane. The sharp sound of the buzzer startled her as it released the lock, Raegan strode up the two flights of stairs having to retrieve her breath as she reached the top. She had approached this door many times in her life but there was a distinct difference this time. The space felt calmer, warmer than this morning, the front door opened to reveal her Gran sitting radiant in the room, from a distance Raegan noted her sparkling complexion and glistening aura, she looked delicate, like crystal gemstones. Raegan stopped in the doorway overwhelmed by her reflexion in the hall mirror, she too was glowing, the light covered her body from top to toe. She carefully stepped forward to inspect.

'I told you I needed to talk to you dear' said her Gran from behind her. Raegan stood captivated at her reflection,

'What is it?' she said under her breath,

'It's Glimmer dear' her Gran replied,

'Glimmer?' said Raegan staring straight through the mirror. Something felt different, like a weight had been lifted from her shoulders, the pressure that had lay deep for so long had evaporated, she   felt   reborn.

CHAPTER 6

DAWN

18 years earlier

Dawn sat peering over her newspaper, she wasn't actually reading it but had picked it up for the hype on the sports page, she wasn't really a sports fan. Shaylock was hot in June, not just warm but hot, the sort of heat that clung to you, invading each orifice indignantly. She slurped her ice cream soda, the cold creamy bubbles filling her mouth, she was never going to grow out of these. Dawn had accepted her change at sixteen years old, slightly early for a Glimmer but she had coped, she had a strong Vine to support her. The flickers got easier with experience, at first she struggled to separate other people's emotions from her own, often ending up a profuse wreck after just a trip to the mall. Now she could filter it, even use it to her advantage, what felt like a curse before was now a blessing. Her stomach churned, it was so loud she was convinced the sound was echoing through the jukebox, she clung to her abdomen composing herself, inhaling a deep breath to shift it. A flicker from the man on the table to her left circulated Dawn, it was starting to invade her space, usually she could control it but recently her defence beacon was failing, her ability to block the sensations was becoming hit and miss. Still peering over the paper Dawn opened up to the flicker, the man was lonely, he had lost his wife the previous year, his heart was broken and she could feel the two parts desperate to join together again. Most flickers were quick, with only a few seconds of exposure you had everything you needed. You could see directly into the person's soul, from their deepest fears and desires to what they were planning to eat that night. Managing a flicker took practice and was not something that came easily to Dawn, at first she denounced her Glimmer, at just sixteen the last thing she wanted to be was different, but denouncement was painful and draining and it couldn't be upheld for long.

Being a Glimmer is not something you choose, it chooses you. Anyone can be chosen to carry a Glimmer, if you are part of a Vine you are more likely to carry it, but it can happen to anyone. Dawn could remember the heartfelt words her mother had spoken to her before she accepted her Glimmer '*In darkness even a speck of light can be blinding*' ten words that would forever dwell in her thoughts. Dawn wanted to be that spec of light in a world full of darkness, she wanted to make a difference and to help others. What Dawn didn't expect from this insightful excerpt was how much darkness there was and how small the Glimmers of light would seem within it. She focussed hard trying to interpret what would make the old man happy again, she couldn't fix him, she wasn't powerful enough for that, but she could steer him in the right direction. He sat frozen, eyes fixated on his bacon and pancakes, they were probably cold, and he had hardly touched them. Dawn looked down at her hands fidgeting for an answer, as she pondered a yellow bannered advert in the paper caught her eye, she quickly ripped the bottom of the page and stuffed it in her jacket pocket. As she casually walked over to the cashier to pay the bill she wedged the off cut in her hand, Dawn moved cautiously towards the exit trying not to raise suspicion, outside an odd looking character was poised against the window to greet her, over chewing his gum and trying to look casual.

'They in there?' the stranger asked,

'Yeah, but wait' Dawn replied in anticipation. The pair glared through the window

'Look, watch' said Dawn eagerly as she watched the waitress deliver the man the bill with the scrappy cut off advert on the tray, the man looked around puzzled by the gift as if aware that someone had trespassed his thoughts. He retrieved a pair of bifocals from his upper breast pocket and carefully read the note. Dawn stood motionless awaiting his reaction, this is the part she is at her most vulnerable, to the naked eye she can be seen literally glowing.

'Hey Dawn, stop it, we're gonna get sprung if you carry on like this',

She covered his mouth with her hand as he whispered the last word under his breath. The old man's eye line regained its natural position and he let out a thankful sigh whilst a small, knowing smile assembled on his aged face. Dawn's job was done. She let the warm moment caress her, being a Glimmer wasn't about her own feelings but when a flicker has been crowned there was an enormous sense of triumph, but her moment ended abruptly.

'Hey, they're leaving' he said,

Angelo and Dawn were consorts, bonded together by their Glimmer ranks. He was slightly older than Dawn, but his change hadn't occurred until he was nineteen. Being from an immigrant family Angelo didn't have the Vine links that Dawn did, no one in his immediate family had a Glimmer, his Vine was deeper than direct relations. He had a tough time accepting his gift, spent six months in juvey on mental health grounds before he finally accepted it. It was Sandy, Dawns mother who found him and taught him the ways. Angelo had become her consort because they were both Steerers, middle rank Glimmers. Steerers had the ability to read flickers and steer people in the right direction, just small things that could change someone's life for the better. Dawn's auntie Meryl was a watcher, her gift was not as stable as Dawn and Angelo so she could not nurture direct contact with people's emotions, Watchers are the most common rank, they can only guide people to make good choices and be there to support people in times of need, so Dawn was proud to be more than that. The third rank of Glimmer was the least common and Dawn didn't know anyone who possessed that level of gift. Her mother had told her stories of one Glimmer she knew of, enchanted stories that would fill up her heart and leave her yearning for more. These first-degree Glimmers were called Mappers. Mappers had the ability to remap lives, to both look into people's souls and directly influence their cognitive processes. It was the gift of thought manipulation, sometimes known as inception; the craft of planting a seed and watching it grow. From what Dawn had been told although this was an elusive gift it was also immensely dangerous, one of the reasons Mappers were uncommon was because they didn't last as long as others, their gift could be erratic, lacked control and the consequences for bad choices were worse, a lot worse.

Angelo signalled Dawn to duck as two tall dark figures exited the diner. They glided out of the glass doorway carrying an air of arrogance as they walked down the sidewalk towards 23rd street. Dawns eyes locked on the two Leon's, *'to fulfil the Glimmer prophecy one must eradicate the darkness that suppresses lights true form'* the words rang clear in her ears as she trailed the two young men. Dawn was not hiding from the pair, she knew they could sense her, it was a mutual kinetic perception that had been shared by Glimmer and Leon for generations. Neither Leon turned around the entire two kilometre walk; they didn't run or try to dodge them, just kept walking. Dawn was tired, she had been on her feet for hours, the sun was slowly descending in the sky but the heat was still sticky beneath her neck, light headedness had plagued her all day and this long trek was not helping.

'We can't go much further' said Angelo

The light in the sky was fading and the density of the darkness was starting to dominate the neo suburban townscape. Dawn knew she could only go so far, but she was always tempted to push it. The terrain was different on this side of town, the buildings were taller, vaster, a myriad of windows looked upon a trail of dimly lit backstreets. Dawn could feel the change in the air. An intense pain drenched her; this was a harsh place to live. Any closer and both Glimmers would trigger a tsunami of sadness coming their way. Just before she turned to head home the Leon's altered their course and began to retrace their steps striding confidently towards them. Her heart skipped a beat watching them return their way.

'You looking to join us this evening Dawn?' said the tallest of the two men,

'I was contemplating it' said Dawn in her usual sarcastic way.

'Why are you stalking us Glimmer?'

'Just checking on your intentions, we know how you can stray' Angelo butted in. The conversation had taken a sobering turn as Kane and his consort Hayes circled them like vultures.

'I think you two should go, you can see we made it home safely' said Kane teasing the duo. Angelo stepped forward; Dawn mirrored his movement.

'Come on we've done our bit' she said hoping to defuse the situation,

'Unless you're staying to see Devin' replied Hayes, stirring the pot. Dawn choked silently unable to find the words to reply. Angelo's eyes perforated hers throwing a thousand probing questions without a single word leaving his lips.

'I take that as a no then...well they do say three is a crowd!', Hayes continued nodding towards his comrade, the pair exited the path disappearing into the urban void.

It is a good thing Glimmers couldn't read each other, the silence on the journey home was agonizing enough. Angelo marched two paces in front as if leading a naughty teenager home. The quiet was raw, throbbing in her head, she wanted to explain but her words would fall on deaf ears, there was nothing she could say to fix this. As she turned back onto 23rd street she looked up at the row of lit windows, she longed for the simpler days when her biggest worry was completing homework and what would be for supper that night. A cold shiver surged through her body making her senses heighten, for a moment she imagined his hands on her waist pulling her tight towards him, his breath warm on the nape of her neck, their lips carefully caressing each other as his eyes swallowed her enticing her into his darkness. Her heated daze ended abruptly with Angelo's first word to her.

'Dawn, get in here it's freezing',

Composing herself and locking away her thoughts Dawn complied and entered the building. This evening mess had made her nauseous, her stomach bubbled softly as she reached the top of the stairwell. Angelo blocked her entrance to the hallway,

'We are going to talk about his' he stated, sounding like a disappointed father,

'Okay okay' she said pushing through his arms. The nausea forced itself higher into her gullet now; she took deep breaths to try and control it.

'Evening you two, how was your......' her mother had barely started her sentence when Dawn barged into the bathroom, grasped edges of the toilet bowl and was greeted by her ice cream soda, maybe she would grow out of these.

CHAPTER 7

RAEGAN

The next morning Raegan couldn't stop looking at her reflection, she had been staring at herself for hours trying to digest what her Gran had told her, she had endless questions cascading through her mind. Carefully opening the bedroom door, she peaked through the gap trying to remain invisible so not to cause a disturbance, she tip-toed towards the bathroom avoiding the creaks in the old floor when a voice came abruptly from the living room.

'I am awake dear' said her Gran sitting regally in her armchair,

'You can come and sit with me if you like'. Raegan had so many questions but part of her was still sceptical about last night's revelations, she huddled herself into a tight ball on the couch.

'Did you sleep well?' her Gran asked with a hint of ridicule in her voice,

Only then did it dawn on Raegan how well she had slept, not a single abnormal dream or episode, no hot flushes or attacks of insomnia, just pure sleep. She sat for a moment hugging her knees into her chest as a sign of her new insecurity; her Gran sat patiently waiting for the first word to leave her lips.

'Was she like me?' she said looking into her hands to avoid making eye contact.

A moment passed before her Gran replied as she was painfully searching through the files in her head to find the right answer.

'What does your heart tell you?' Her eyes stayed down; Raegan stared at the creases in her hands tracing the lines with her fingers thinking about the question her Gran had posed. Her Gran stumbled over and sat close beside her, taking her hand and resting her index finger on her palm.

'You see all of these lines Rae, deep long ones with small branches coming from them, all interconnecting with one another',

Raegan's brow creased as she looked on intently,

'These lines are like your gift; you are one of the branches of course' she smiled to herself.

'Glimmer families work on Vines so most people who are on the Vine will be a Glimmer'

Raegan sat pondering on that point for a moment before she replied.

'So, if I am a Glimmer and you are a Glimmer then she must have been one' Raegan stated methodically, she wasn't sure if this disclosure was making the water clearer or muddier but pressure was building up in her gut, hot and fiery like a dragon brewing a mighty roar.

'Is it how she died?' Raegan asked more confidently this time,

'It's complicated dear', her Gran shut off unexpectedly.

The mood of the room had changed, a dark cloud had descended, there was a distinct sense of danger looming. Raegan sat frozen on the couch staring directly ahead, she had heard each cutting word of the reply but had not acknowledge them; she worked through each letter, but they did not make sense. She turned to face her Gran holding out a peace flag to show that the passageway was safe to enter. The words left her lips again but this time with more vigour.

'Is it how she died?'

She could feel a storm of aggression begin to build, she wanted an answer, she deserved an answer.

'As I said dear, it's complicated' replied her Gran more forcefully this time.

The two words struck deep and wounded Raegan for the second time, she jumped up from the couch grabbing her Grans lower arms tightly.

'I need this Gran, I need you to tell me',

A dark energy ran through Raegan's body, not heavy and thick like before but fluid and surging at the speed of light. The lights in the apartment began to quiver as Raegan grew impatient with the secrecy. She caught a glimpse of her Gran, wide eyed mix of intrigue and fear in her face.

'Being a Glimmer isn't what killed her Rae, but it was why she left us....I don't know anything else' she said

'I can't help you Rae, it's too painful, she was my baby and I lost her',

Tears began to roll down her face. Raegan released her grip letting her Gran fall back onto the couch, her breath was shallow as she rested against the cushion, Raegan scrambled out of the room and slammed the door. She pressed her back into the wall slowly plummeting to the floor, her head in her hands and her eyes closed tight.

'What just happened?' she reprimanded herself,

'Why did I do that?' she scolded

Glimmers are supposed to be kind and hopeful, what had come over her? The guilt lay heavy as she lifted herself from the floor, a message alert flashed on her phone 'U COMING 2DAY? – Alice' short, sweet and to the point, school was the last place she wanted to go but staying here wasn't an option.

CHAPTER 8

RAEGAN

Raegan had not appreciated how challenging just walking down the street could be as a Glimmer, her head filled with dozens of lucid images cast out by their hosts. The busyness made her head feel fuzzy, clouded by expelled visions; she barely made it to Alice's house. As she stumbled towards the driveway, she noticed Alice standing anxiously awaiting her arrival. Raegan continued towards her cautiously glancing around her like a Russian spy.

'Hey, what's with the drama?' said Alice with a heightened tone in her voice,

'The whole school is talking about you. You're like the big news!',

'Great!' replied Raegan,

'And that's why we are not going to school today' she said semi aggressively.

'Playing hooky! Rae what has got into you...is it that boy...? Are you hiding something from…'?

Raegan stopped her mid-sentence and moved close to her face.

'I'll fill you in later, we just need to get out of here'.

'Ok, I know a place, my cousin works there; she won't ask any questions',

'Lead the way'.

*   *   *   *

The diner had seen better days, the building itself was still intact but the shell ached for some filler and paint, the external walls crumbled in the soft wind leaving gaping holes in the paintwork, the neon red sign that rested above the door was missing its final letter so read 'DINE' and resembled something you expect to see in red light district, but for all of its flaws it was barely occupied and served coffee so it would do. Alice appeared to be enjoying this special trip, barricading them both in the booth with the encrusted diner menus like two escaped convicts. Raegan look a deep breath, the first real one of the morning. The diner was deserted with only a few lone wolves sipping coffee and eating pancakes at the bar. Raegan was starting to understand that it was the lone wolves that were the most dangerous for her, sat mulling over their failed lives and bad decisions. People that are busy and have distracted minds and do not ponder upon their life as regularly as lone wolves, Raegan needed to keep her distance to avoid any issues today.

'What can I get you girls?' said the waitress, she was young, slightly scraggy, her limited time on earth had obviously been hard on her,

'I'll have a black coffee' said Alice trying to usher the waitress away as quickly as possible.

'An ice cream soda please' Raegan said gratefully, staring blankly at the menu trying to avoid direct eye contact - a sugar hit would be welcomed after the twenty-four hours she had just been through. As the waitress moved away Raegan could feel her thoughts and feelings trying to penetrate her mind, she didn't trust herself to cope with it all yet, so she pushed to block it all out. Eventually the feelings subsided, and she became conscious of her surroundings again.

'Rae, Rae?' Alice's voice was escalating

'Where did you go?', Raegan sat slightly disorientated by the encounter but relieved that she managed to control it.

'What's up with you Rae?', What is all of this about? What happened to you yesterday?'

Endless questions were tumbling out of Alice's mouth, Raegan lost track of which one to answer first,

'It's complicated...' the two words only an hour before she had despised were now her only answer.

'Ok, let's tackle this bit by bit' said Alice signalling downwards with both her hands.

'Firstly, why did you look so pained when we ordered, are you sick?' Raegan huffed humorously under her breath,

'No, I'm not sick....' She paused fidgeting the menu in her hands.

'You remember when I said my Gran was getting all serious and meaningful and I was dodging her calls and texts',

'Yeah'

'Well, turns out, if I would have listened yesterday's little drama could have been avoided'

Raegan paused reflecting on the incident and imagining what the student body must have thought.

'Turns out your psychic Sal estimation wasn't far out'

Alice looked at Raegan perplexed, the cogs in her brain slowly processing the information.

'Are you psychic, like you talk to dead people and stuff?'

'NO! I'm not like a medium or anything, I can just, sort of, read people...I guess...', Alice paused contemplating Raegan's last sentence.

'You can tell what I am thinking right now? Ok, go on then' she taunted 'What am I thinking right now?'

'It doesn't work like that Alice, geez, I thought you might understand or at least hear me out!'

Silence lingered over the table as the waitress brought their drinks.

'Would you like anything else? Asked the waitress glancing impatiently towards the list of orders on the cash register,

'No' Raegan said, wishing her to leave the table, the waitress rolled her eyes and tottered off.

'So, what has this got to do with your Gran?' asked Alice,

'Turns out it's not a random occurrence but something that runs in families or as she calls it 'Vines'

Raegan thought that conveying the information to someone else would help her make sense of it but all it was doing was throwing up more unanswered questions.

'How does it work? You can just see into everyone's minds? Can you make things move? Do you have superpowers?

Alice's list continued with an excited pitch shift to her voice, the conversation was drifting into dangerous territory.

'I don't really know the in's and out's yet' she replied as she slurped her melted ice cream soda.

Alice pondered over her next bout of questions.

'Why are we ditching school today? I'm sure your psycho-drama from yesterday is old news, you know how fickle the social circles are' said Alice rolling her eyes trying to lighten the mood. Raegan stared at the dregs of ice cream that had settled in the bottom of the glass, her mind was wondering, she kept reliving yesterday with Dom, was he like her? Is that why they had a connection? But the connection felt wrong, like water with electricity, the power and spark were there; but it was dangerous. Raegan knew it was dangerous.

'Well we can't stay here all day!' Alice shrugged interrupting Raegan's train of thought

'I can only drink so much coffee'.

Raegan hadn't thought that far ahead,

'Your house?', Alice's parents were barely even home after school no matter mid-morning,

'Damn no' Alice cursed

'The maid is in cleaning today, if I turn up at the house it will definitely get back to my parents…your Grans?'

'Nope, reading group meeting', both girls slumped into the booth reminiscing over their poorly organised plans. The bell rang at the front counter and it sent shudders down Raegan's spine. Alice was glued to her cell phone trying to remedy their 'hooky' misjudgement, the bell rang again, this time impatiently.

'Give the woman a break! 'said Raegan under her breath. She turned to investigate who the demanding person was when Alice grabbed her hand and pulled her towards the edge of the table. Raegan was confused for a moment recovering from the shock of what had just happened, Alice was listening intently with her head flat against the stained coffee cup.

'What are....' said Raegan,

'Shhhhhh' signalled Alice holding her semi painted nail against her lips. It didn't take Raegan long to revive the empty feeling that had entered her space only hours before. Her intuition had refined itself in the past twenty-four hours and she was now in tune with it. It was Dom that Alice had seen, Raegan could feel it, her sharp reflexes had given her time to strategize and her strategy was simple, stay hidden. Dom's eyes scoured the diner looking past the empty booths, his eyes fixed on a deserted table that had not been cleared. Raegan could feel his frustration; it was climaxing like a fireball inside his stomach.

'Can I help you?' the young pretty waitress asked

'No, you're good' he replied forcefully banging his fist on the bar and sharply exiting the diner.

'Has he gone?' Alice whispered

'I think so'

'How did you know to hide from him? I thought he was going to be your future husband?'

Raegan joked as she pushed her way back up to a respectable position,

'Well, it didn't take much to realise that there is something off with you guys, I know you haven't shared the details yet' she paused in anticipation

'But you will. Now we really need to get out of here and we need to avoid any common hangouts'.

CHAPTER 9

RAEGAN

They had been rambling around for hours chatting about idle things trying to avoid the big topic that Alice was craving details of. It wasn't long before the bright afternoon sun started to dip in the sky, Raegan stared at her elongated shadow as she drifted aimlessly across the green park. The air was fresh and whipped around blowing her cobwebs away. Raegan's phone vibrated in her jacket pocket, the message was from her Gran 'Home for tee tonight?' it read, the autocorrect made Raegan smile as she swiped the screen to dismiss the reply box.

'Shall we keep going?' Alice asked subtlety nodding back towards town,

'No, not yet, let's keep going, if we're home too early they will get suspicious',

'Good point' Alice agreed.

The park was becoming desolate as the girls walked through, its fluffy green grass turned into stiff yellow straw and the ground became broken and uneven. As they reached the fringe of the park the high-rise tower block hid the sun from view. The buildings in this area of town were a lot higher than where Raegan and Alice lived, there were so many windows looking onto the street, like a thousand laser beams fixing on them searching for a target.

'Don't you think we should be turning around about now?' said Alice in a slightly concerned tone.

Raegan felt the same but couldn't shake off the impulse to go further, her feet kept taking slow, calculated steps into the urban jungle. Hesitantly, Alice kept up with Raegan, eyes wide to take in the new landscape. Raegan was aware of how out of place she looked this side of town, but a magnetic force pulled her deeper into the slum. The streets looked similar to her side of town, just unkempt and unloved. The tall buildings prevented most of the late afternoon sun from hitting the roadway, just slithers of natural light lay solitary on the tarmac. Alice began to pull on Raegan's jacket sleeve, willing her to turn around and retreat from the shadowy street.

'Rae, what's the plan?' a slight quiver plaguing Alice's voice.

Raegan wasn't ignoring her, but her voice was drowned out by a cascade of anger gushing towards her in a stampede; this was not a happy place. Raegan was overwhelmed by the sheer measure of the misery that unfolded before her. Every light in every window told a different story. The streets were deserted by the time they reached

Central Avenue, only a scattering of people still lined the sidewalks. Raegan's gaze was drawn towards a short man carting a crate of Budweiser on the other side of the street, the bottles rattled furiously as he walked, like he was forcing them to make the sound. The man was about 5'8'', short hair, slightly balding in the middle, probably about forty years old, his waistline had definitely seen younger years. Robotically he carried each crate from the van making a 'umpf' sound as he lifted them. Raegan looked on as he repeated the same motion two or three times before he caught her eye. His eyes were speckled brown and hidden between heavy eyelids. He carried his troubles in his eyes, his discontent with life was evident in the way he moved, there was no rush or impetus, just never-ending time. Raegan could feel herself being pulled towards him, not in a physical sense but his presence was growing into her space. It happened in less than thirty seconds; a detailed illustration inscribed its way into her mind. She stood immobile, transfixed by the hundreds of obscure images, individually making no sense but when thrown together telling a bitter tale. She leapt from image to image trying to make out what he was showing her, the images formed an uncomfortable plateau in her mind, something was out of sorts, something felt wrong. The bottles continued to rattle excitedly in the crate, eager to see how she would respond, their constant chatter heightening Raegan's unease. She felt sad for the man, from what she could see he lived a minimal life, surviving on the periphery of existence, merely trying to earn a wage to send his young daughter to school. Over the past year his gambling debts had got too much, and his wife had left him, Raegan could feel his broken heart and overwhelming sorrow for what he had lost. She could feel the emptiness that burned inside him, she imagined an emotional reunion, like at the end of a slushy movie. He would dramatically drop the heavy crate and dart home to beg for forgiveness and to reconcile with his wife. Raegan could see the tears falling from her eyes and feel the warmth they shared when they were together. In a movie the music would have built up to a dramatic crescendo climaxing as the reformed lovers shared a kiss.

Lost in her dream Raegan was unaware of the action happening directly before her. The breath-taking crescendo that was playing out in her mind was broken by an almighty crash of glass smashing down on the hard tarmac. The amber liquid spread quickly on the ground forming a dangerous puddle of pungent glass and ale, the smell wafted towards Raegan as she watched the man run rapidly down the sidewalk; for a moment she could not link the two scenes together, she stood paralysed meters away from the dangerous puddle as the full extent of what was happening dawned on her. He had seen it too. Before she had the chance to speak a blood curdling scream left Alice's mouth followed by a merciless thump. He didn't see it coming, he wouldn't have known it was coming, it wasn't part of the scene. Raegan looked forward at what was unfolding at the end of the street, the truck driver sat distraught with his with his head in his hands at the side of the road as hordes of passers-by looked on at the bloody sight. He didn't stand a chance. Raegan hadn't taken a breath for a few seconds, she struggled to let air in.

Did she do that? If so, how? Her breath returned thick and fast as the gravity of the situation struck her. Alice pulled Raegan backwards aware of what had just occurred. Her cell phone was vibrating in her top pocket, it rang three, four times before it cut out; Raegan knew who it was. Chaos slowly revealed itself as two suspicious figures appeared from the shadows heading straight towards them in thick calculated steps.

'It can't be' uttered Raegan under her breath as the distance between them closed in.

Raegan's feet were concreated to the ground, whether it was through fear or grief she knew she had to escape. She could hear Alice begging her to move, pleading with her hysterically to leave with so much vigour that she had pulled the jacket clean from her back. Raegan was lost in all the confusion, her vision blurred as her eyes filled with tears, disorientation swirled around her like a tornado. It stopped; a rush of energy pulsed through her hand as Dom pulled her back to her senses making her heart race.

'We have to get away from here' shouted Dom gasping for breath, Raegan was unsure if this was part of her dream or if it was really happening,

'You shouldn't be here, it's not safe' he continued.

Running down Central Avenue and clearing the back of the park, Raegan heard the sirens whirring as they approached the grim scene, her mind replaying a single image over and over, she could feel her legs running away but her mind was still at the scene trying to piece together what had happened. As they reached park the street lamps were buzzing to come on, Dom stopped dead.

'I'll leave you here, you should be safe now, they won't come this far out, but go straight home' he said with an unnatural urgency.

Raegan stared back at him, eyes dead, overwhelmed by what had just happened. He left them stranded in the park, shock screeching in their ears as they worked out the next move. She needed to get to her Gran, she needed to explain, she needed answers, what had she done? What had she done? As she raced back towards the safety of her Grans a single image lurked in her mind. A young girl smiled sweetly into the camera, gap-toothed with ragged hair falling gently onto her shoulders...What had she done?

CHAPTER 10

DAWN

Dawn stared at the mountains of papers on her desk, her morning was going by slowly, every time she looked at the clock it had hardly moved. White mulch covered her desk, only a few checkered spaces remained free, she could barely see the cherry oak wood. Dawn was usually very organised, that's why she was so good at her job, her desk had never been so disorderly. Dawn visualised the mess as a metaphor for her current life. She glanced again at the clock, another minute had ticked past, rattling her fingers over the keyboard she tried to kick herself into gear. The phone bleeped impatiently as Dawn composed herself ready for the call,

'Good morning, welcome to Tigar Barton, how can I assist you today?'

She had worked for the partners for three years, the job was mediocre, it had its up and downs, but it was something she enjoyed and thrived on. Rachel Tigar and Tim Barton were family mediation lawyer's, the practice was small but extremely effective. The building sat central in the town directly above the best bakers in town. Just a simple glass frontage stating the brand name was all that advertised the practice but as the mountain on the desk suggested the work wasn't drying up anytime soon. As Dawn listened intently to the stranger on the phone her nostrils were filled with a sweet pastry drifting up from the bakery, her usual approach was to fill her lungs with the heavenly aroma and hope that Franco would grace them with some cut offs or tit bits from the morning bake. This morning was altogether different, the smell turned her stomach upside down, her throat closed tight trying to hold down the milky coffee she had drank only thirty minutes earlier.

'Well can I take your details?' she said trying to suppress the nausea filling her mouth.

'Excellent, thank you, we'll get back to you as soon as we can',

The call ended abruptly as Dawn held her head in her hands taking in short sharp breaths.

'You ok Dawn?' mouthed her concerned colleague whilst still maintaining her phone conversation, Dawn nodded covering her mouth with her hand. She reached for the empty water bottle hidden underneath the papers, a dribble of water lay stagnant in the bottom, but Dawn couldn't be fussy. As the morning dragged on the nausea lifted leaving a grumbling sensation inside her stomach, the clock hit one o clock faster than she had imagined and she made her way down to the street front to order her usual cheese and bacon sub. The line was never long but the delicious smell made the delay go on forever. As Dawn waited patiently third in line, she could feel a flicker coming on, her beacon had been off recently, only providing semi flickers and not telling her the whole story. She could not work out who's flicker it was, the images were muddled, and she didn't recognise any of the blurred faces. As the images infused together, she barely made out the basics of the life story, she couldn't help, she couldn't see enough to help. Failure to remedy or support for a Glimmer was crushing and felt poisonous, this failure would hang over her for a day or so, draining her natural glow and weakening her senses. Dawn felt like this most of the time now anyway, she couldn't shift the weight that lay heavy on her shoulders. Making her way to the front of the line she lost her appetite, even adding the infamous meatball sauce couldn't tempt her now.

'Just a water' she said feeling sorry for herself.

Leaving the bakery empty handed was painful but necessary, sipping her water she slowly meandered up the street towards the high school. She could hear the buzz of unfulfilled hopes and dreams before she turned the corner. So many prospects, unknown journeys and daring feats awaited them, she wished herself back to that time. Dawn enjoyed school, she was a good student, smart, sporty and popular, until her sophomore year when her Glimmer kicked in, everything got harder after that and she started to fall in with the less desirable kids in the neighbourhood. That was where she met him. Dawn ambled back towards her office kicking her heels against the pavement as she walked, only meters from the office door a tall, built, handsome man skulked in the backstreet. Dawn knew he was there before she saw him; that sense hadn't faded. He shifted uncomfortably waiting for her join him, she was a secret he couldn't share.

'Hey, you' he said warmly reaching his hand towards her affectionately.

'Hey' she replied keeping an appropriate distance,

'What's up?'

'You know what's up! you know it's difficult Dev, and it has been even worse since your crony opened his big mouth in front of Angelo' her annoyance filled the space between them.

'Yeah I heard, what did Angelo say? I take it from Kane it wasn't well received' he said with a smirk to his voice.

Dawn scowled; daggers flew towards him but landed in a pile by his feet as he gazed apologetically into her eyes.

'It's not funny Dev, you never take this stuff seriously, if my Mom finds out I could be dispelled by my Vine, rejected by my family and everyone who loves me' Dawn stared down toward the littered ground.

'Everyone but me...' he replied taking the opportunity to comfort her.

Moving forward into her space he grasped both hands intertwining their fingers as one, she could feel his breath brush her forehead as he leaned down towards her.

'Dawn, come on, none of that matters, there is no proof we even know each other, for all Angelo knows Kane was just trying to stir things up'

He moved closer pressing his strong torso into hers.

'Dawn' he whispered as he nestled his nose into her forehead longing for a response. Dawn breathed him in, he was enchanting, every cell of him captivated her, she felt drunk in his presence. Accepting defeat, she surrendered to his plea meeting his lips with hers, his face wasn't as smooth as it looked, a short rebellious stubble brushed her chin as their lips grazed each other tenderly. Part of his appeal was in his strength, he always held her with such confidence, such power, every move he made was purposeful. The other part was the darkness that surrounded him, it was addictive, she craved it and felt compulsed to seek it out. As Devin moved his hand to caress her cheek Dawn broke away tuning herself back into the real world.

'I've got to get back...' she said as she stepped away,

He grasped her hand tighter as she backed away longing to hold on to the embrace for another second. Dawn could feel her lunch break ticking quickly away and did not want to enter the office late again.

'Meet me later then?'

Dawn wanted to decline his request but found it difficult to do, she would need to sneak out under another premise and that had got a lot more challenging recently with Angelo watching her every move. Feeling powerless she nodded as he released her hand, it felt moist and clammy as the midday air wrapped around it. Devin disappeared silently into the shadows, holding her gaze until the last moment; as a teenager she struggled to understand the girls that were besotted by boys, she couldn't comprehend how they could be so attached to one person and make themselves so detached from the rest of humanity. It had happened to several of her friends as she grew up, their worlds seemed centred around just one person, like a spell had been cast upon them. At fifteen years old it had seemed alien to her but now Dawn knew how it felt, her main problem was that in her world her love for Devin was forbidden, no one could know their secret, it was imperative that what they had stayed between them. There would never be a big unveiling, no family dinners, there would be no happy ending, but Dawn didn't care, what they had was stronger than any of the that.

Skulking back to the office Dawn was deflated by her brisk encounter, something didn't feel right, it sat heavy in her gut. Approaching the mountain of work on the table she huffed, if only she could shift this sinking feeling in the pit of her stomach, it made it hard to focus. As her working day drew to a close her eyelids drooped heavily, to the naked eye her desk didn't look very different from when she arrived that morning but she had made progress, focussing on clearing the work helped to distract her from thinking about Devin, thinking about Angelo and thinking about her ailing stomach. She left the office with a justified sense of satisfaction.

Turning the corner Dawn looked lovingly up at the light shining bright from her Mom's window, it always seemed to be the brightest in the street; she could feel the warmth radiating from the apartment. She walked towards the building catching a glance of two figures, one soft smiling face waving excitedly at her and the other an untrusting squint watching carefully as she entered the building. The elevator never worked in the apartment building so Dawn had got used to staggering up the stairs. Upon entering Angelo's eyes combed her body top to toe for evidence of her day's endeavours, nothing was the same now, just a shrewd comment from a Leon crony was enough to raise his suspicions. Before, when he would enquire to her whereabouts during the day, she could stumble around small lies, or as she would call them, inaccuracies. She was at lots of the places she told Angelo, she just missed out the small detail about the company she kept.

'Evening darling' said her Mom,

'Are you ok? you look a little peaky?' her Mom pressed the back of her hand onto Dawns forehead feeling for a fever.

'I'm fine' said Dawn as two cold hands moved down to her lymph nodes,

'I've just had a crazy busy day; I should just get my head down...'

Dawns mum clasped her hands together and gestured towards Angelo who was standing waiting in the dining area.

'But Angelo's come to see you' she said encouragingly.

'He wanted to check you were ok as you were out of the office at lunch today when he called, he thought you might have come home sick'.

'Stupid Rita!' Dawn cursed under her breath,

'Rita said you didn't feel great and had taken a slightly longer lunch break to get some fresh air...I was just worried' he said through gritted teeth.

Much of the conversation Dawn and Angelo were having was non-verbal, he glared at her with a wicked stare, his words spoken with an accusative tone. Not wanting to break eye contact Dawn stepped forward bridging the gap between the two of them and making herself dominant in the space.

'Yeah, I did feel a little flush, so I took a longer lunch to refresh my head',

There was no lie there, it is what happened, she just left out one tiny detail.

'Good, well I'm glad to see you are okay now' Angelo replied, obviously not believing a word she said. The pair held each other's gaze until her mom broke the silence.

'We'll see you tomorrow then dear'.

Her Mom ushered Angelo towards the door and turned to Dawn hoping for some sort of explanation as to why the two consorts were having communication problems.

'Thank you for your concern Angelo dear, I'm sure she will be feeling more like herself soon',

Before she could finish her sentence, the door shut abruptly not leaving Angelo anytime to reply. Her Mom stood in the doorway staring straight at Dawn, the silence held for a few seconds before the onslaught of questions pounced forward at her.

'Angelo seems concerned about something' she thrust forward with an untrusting tone,

'You two do not seem to be getting on at the minute, there is a rather large and rather protruding elephant in the room'.

Dawn rolled her eyes flippantly feeling like a delinquent teenager again.

'We are just in a disagreement at the moment, nothing sinister, just a small misunderstanding',

She didn't want to invite anymore unnecessary questions, so she spoke clearly and concisely as if she was giving her closing statement in a court room. Dawn slowly edged sideways trying to escape to the sanctuary of her room, but each step was counteracted, the pair resembling two tango dancers.

'So, you have nothing to share with me then? her Mom probed taking another swift step to the side.

'Have you had any flickers lately? Were they successful?' she said,

The questions continued coming think and fast.

'No, my flickers have been off recently, I think it is this stomach flu I have been fighting off',

Dawn rubbed her lower abdomen to accentuate the statement. Another uncomfortable silence came over the pair, her mother looked up smiling from ear to ear.

'Ok dear' she replied changing her tone from inquisition to illusive.

'Get some rest and we can look to sort you out in the morning...I'll assemble the Vine to see if we can stimulate your Glimmer from within' she said decisively.

'Really, I don't think...' cut off mid-sentence, her plea fell on deaf ears.

Whilst her Mom scurried around searching for her phone directory Dawn moved silently into her bedroom longing for its solace, she closed the door and clicked the small gold lock mechanism, the breath left her body, relieved for just a moment to have steered clear for another day, but she couldn't go on like this. The sections of her life were beginning to collide, they were no longer separate, and she was losing control of all of them. There was no way she could leave her flat tonight, even if she made it past her Mom, she knew Angelo would be lurking close by to catch her out. Her head was spinning at one hundred miles per hour with three people all trying to push her out of the driving seat. Perching at the end of her bed she looked out onto the street wondering what complication others had in their lives. The clock read 6.15pm, she wouldn't even be able to contact Devin, he would wait twenty minutes then leave thinking she had just stood him up. Dawns stomach sank at the thought; she didn't want to hurt him but lately that was all that she seemed to do. Throwing her head back onto the mattress her hair settled over her forehead, she recalled the moment she fell in love with Devin, the exact moment calved eternally into her heart. Closing her eyes, she felt his torso firm on hers, his skin smooth and tanned, his warm breath lingering as he whispered in her ear. The intensity of their souls entwined together for a moment of shared ecstasy, she thought it was a cliché but at that moment she knew she was in love.

CHAPTER 11

DAWN

The morning came quickly; Dawns head had barely hit the pillow when she was awoken by the sunlight shining through the crack in the blind. Her sleep although fleeting, was soothing, her head felt clearer, her thoughts more defined. Lifting from the pillow Dawn took at long deep yawn going momentarily deaf as it climaxed, she could smell her Mom's herbal tea, but the suffocating scent was soon rivalled by the rich smell of peculator coffee. This was the heavy stuff, it smelt like thick roasted tar and she imagined it didn't taste much better. The coffee was the first indicator that Angelo was present, Dawn understood his persistence, he cared about her, she got it, but it was becoming overwhelming. Three hushed voices mingled in the hallway all talking over one another, Dawn unlatched the door and peeked through the gap, her Mom and Angelo stood either side of a person she did not recognise. The lady was tall, broad (for a woman) with a carefully constructed central pin bob holding her soft white hair in place. From the back Dawn could have mistaken her for a man, only her smart black patent heels and tailored skirt ensured her gender. The women stood facing the opposite door and was being held in place by Angelo as she struggled to hold her own weight. The hallway went quiet as Dawn opened the bedroom door, she felt under dressed for the occasion in her cotton striped pyjamas. Angelo and her Mom looked reassuringly as the large woman turned to face her. The woman's eyes were glazed, she edged closer to Dawn with Angelo navigating her around the unfamiliar environment, she held her hand forward reaching for Dawn. Dawns eyes fixed on her Mom for reassurance, but she simply looked down so not to interfere with the stranger's work.

'Is this not a little over the top for stomach flu?' said Dawn

'Hush dear, let the lady work and you will be right as rain in no time' her Mom replied.

Standing barely a foot away the lady stopped and traced her hands around Dawns face, they smelt like a make-up counter at a department store, a floral uplifting scent clung to them. Dawn grew anxious as the woman stood silently cradling her head in her hands, her senses were heightened, she could hear the humming of engines from down the street, feel the slight moist mist that hung in the morning air, it was a similar feeling to just before she received a flicker. The woman's hands slowly traced her collarbone, warmth radiated from her fingers. If this was part of her Mom's remedy it was a good one, as long as she didn't need to ingest any herbs or potions she could cope. The woman's hands continued down past Dawns chest and settling on her stomach.

'Yes, it is the stomach flu that has been interfering with her Glimmer Ma'am' her mom said softly.

The woman paused hovering her hand just below Dawns navel, through split eyelids Dawn watched the woman's face turn from calm to alarm, she winced pulling her entire body into itself. Her hand begun to shake profusely as Dawn held her breath wondering why the woman looked so pained. She mouthed a word Dawn could barely make out, out of breath she repeated the word over and over almost like a mantra. The two simple syllables would change everything... 'Onus'. The word itself didn't mean anything to Dawn but it obviously meant something to her mother who gasped in response bringing her hands directly in front of her mouth.

'What, What?' Dawn shouted impatiently. A single tear dropped from her mother's eye as she reached forward to clasp her hand.

'You're   pregnant   Dawn'.

CHAPTER 12

RAEGAN

The last six hours were a blur, upon returning to the apartment, Raegan was greeted by a heavy affliction, she was unsure how but the news of the incident had already reached her Gran, the flat was full of condemning eyes, the stares sent shivers down her spine. Raegan hadn't spoken a word since her return, she sat quietly in the corner of the bustling room watching the world buzz around her. There were lots of people on cell phones, some pacing the room like they were all miming the same song that nobody could hear. Raegan made herself small in the comfy chair drawing her legs up in-between her arms and placing her head on her knees to drown out the noise. Her head started to thump in the commotion, she hoped that the meeting would finish so she could get some sleep. The image of the little girl lay heavy on her mind, she could still hear the loud crash of the glass against the pavement echoing in her ears, just thinking about the incident made her nauseous. Through the noise a tall, broad shouldered women approached, she knelt down to comfort her.

'Raegan isn't it?' the lady enquired, Raegan nodded without uttering a word,

'I bet this is all very confusing for you' she said, her voice had a European twang to it suggesting to Raegan that this was not her usual place of residence.

'We are not angry with you Raegan, you see, we are just intrigued and what do you say…energised by your troubles'.

After a pause to catch her breath she continued,

'You know we have met before, well sort of anyway',

Raegan looked up at the whimsical lady, she had not noticed before, but her eyes were obscure, moving impulsively by themselves.

'We met when you were just a pup in your Mammy's tum' she said moving in closer. Raegan was intrigued by the woman and her knowledge of her mother, she wanted to question her more but before she could her Gran called silence in the room.

'Hush hush now everybody'.

All eyes were now focussed on her Gran, the room poised for an imminent announcement.

'I think it's time we scale down this meeting and deal with the incident internally' she said glancing over to Rae.

'How can we trust that she can be controlled, we can't have this happening again…' hollered a middle-aged man from the side of the room. Everyone poised waiting intently for his question to be answered. 'Controlled' the word repeated over and over in Raegan's mind, what did they mean controlled?

'This could upset all of the Vines, not just us' another voice bellowed from the back of the room.

'What will happen when the Leon catch on to this predicament, they have as much claim as us!' said another female voice sat directly behind Raegan, she was wearing leather strapped boots with six inch heels and styled purple streaks protruding though her horizontal fringe. Before the woman had time to recover her Gran stormed over and grabbed her by both shoulders, her eyes bulged like hot pokers striking fear through the woman's body. Raegan witnessed her Grans body go physical stiff as she channelled her anger.

'I want to hear no more of this from any of you' she said taking in a deep breath to calm herself down.

'Rae is a Glimmer and it will stay that way, now I kindly ask you all to leave this house and I will attend to the matter with guidance from the higher Vines'.

Without any other questions or even a mutter the crowd exited the cramped flat one by one shooting venomous stares in Raegan's direction. Raegan pondered on the tempered query from the faded rock star, who could have claim? What could they claim? her? how? why? Her mind filled with questions like a cave at high tide. Last to leave was the kind woman who offered her warmth and compassion, as she began to mobilize her Gran moved over to offer her assistance rummaging around the side of the door for her sight stick.

'Don't you worry Rae' she said softly as if she had heard what had been rushing through her mind.

'All things will balance again and remember; darkness can only build when light is not shining true'

Raegan paused for a moment, she was sure there was some deep and significant in her words, but she was too drained to think of it now. Everyone had left, silence plagued the room as her Gran bustled around putting everything back in order. As Raegan stood up to creep out, her Grans voice changed her plans.

'Are we going to discuss what happened today or just pretend it didn't happen?' Raegan would have preferred the latter but knew that it wasn't an actual option.

'I'm just really tired Gran' she said trying to avoid the conversation with a fuzzy head,

'I'm just gonna head back to Dads get some proper rest'

'Your dads not there dear' said her Gran humming around the room making it sound like old news.

'Why? where has he gone?'

'He didn't say dear, just instructed me that you were to stay here with me for a couple of days' she said straightening the coasters on the side table.

'He didn't mention it to me!' Raegan snapped,

'Ah well he did try but you made yourself unavailable for most of the day',

'Well, I need to speak to him'

Raegan grabbed her cell phone and searched impatiently through her contacts.

'He's probably out of range dear, but feel free to leave him a message' said her Gran

Raegan wasn't sure if she was being purposefully aloof or she genuinely had no clue where he was. It was unlike him to leave like this, his phone rang eight times before the voice mail kicked in

'Hey, its Andy, leave a message…'

'Quick and to the point Dad' Raegan muttered before the beep,

'Hey Dad, it's me, Gran just told me you're out of town, so just wanted to check in, call me when you can…love you...'

She wanted to keep it casual so not to raise alarm, she was sure he would call in the morning. Turning to face the door to escape back to her room Raegan noticed her Gran perched in expectation of the conversation she was obviously going to initiate. Raegan sat beside her surrendering to the inevitable, she didn't feel uncomfortable just apprehensive about what she was going to find out.

'Now, I only didn't tell you because I wanted to protect you Rae, you have to understand that before I go any further' she clasped her hand, Raegan was drawn to the smooth crinkled skin that encompassed hers.

'I know now that to protect you I need to bestow all of my knowledge to you' her Gran continued.

Raegan sat back in the chair as her Gran reached forward to the sunset coasters on the small coffee table.

'You see these three coasters' her Gran continued placing them next to each other on the table,

'These represent the different levels of Glimmer'

Carefully picking up the saltshaker she poured a large measure of salt onto the first mat.

'The first level are called Watchers, these Glimmers are the most common and are often mistaken for just good, honest people, they have no power over anyone, they just observe and assist if needed, like the guidance counsellors of society'.

Her Gran moved the saltshaker to the second mat.

'The second level are Steerers' she continued as she poured out a smaller heap of salt,

'These Glimmers are not as common but have a bigger responsibly' she paused in thought for a moment,

'Your mother was a Steerer, as am I' she continued.

'Steerers have the ability to manipulate situations for the better, to help people see things that they might not originally have seen, we can have influence through the links we make based on the flickers we receive. Encouraging someone to join in with something or to reconcile with one another, we have the power to help that process'.

Raegan sat silent, poised suspiciously at the third coaster. The third pile of salt didn't even meet the quota for a 'pile', her Gran tapped the saltshaker carefully onto the back of her hand and counted out four grains of salt.

'The third level are Mappers, these Glimmers are very uncommon, in fact only four have been known of in the last century'

Raegan moved slowly towards the coaster focusing her eyes on the four singular grains.

'Mappers have a great responsibility, and some would say a curse' Raegan's eyes lifted rapidly to meet her Grans.

'Mappers have the power to influence one's thoughts and feelings, to plant and idea or change someone's mind or pattern…the trouble is that it is not as controllable as the other levels'

Raegan's mind started functioning double time, remembering the details from the previous few days.

'When someone's path has been trespassed, unspeakable damage is done, and that person is then known as a devoid…and there is no helping those souls'.

Raegan watched as her Gran carefully placed one more single strand of salt on to the coaster.

'There   were   only   four...until   now'

CHAPTER 13

DAWN

After she found out, days passed but time did not, her mom had busied herself around the house making chit chat when it was only absolutely necessary. She was obviously furious, not at the pregnancy itself but with the deceit. Dawn hadn't confessed to who the father was yet, she was sure her Mom knew something, but she couldn't prove it. Angelo had gone missing too, she hadn't seen him since the incident at the flat, he hadn't visited or called, he was off the grid. She wasn't surprised, he felt betrayed, their relationship had never gone any further than friends or typical consorts but Dawn knew he felt more than that, she saw it in his eyes last year when he first suspected her relationship with Devin. Thinking about Devin made her heart flutter, but not like it used to, a mix of fear and anxiety overwhelmed her, how would he respond to the news? What would he say?

Dawn envisioned two possible scenarios, in the first his eyes would fill up with joyous love for both Dawn and their unborn child, lifting her clean off of the ground in an intense embrace, an iconic happy ever after in a romantic movie. In the second, a shocked and deceived reproach as his eyes searched the ground to avoid eye contact and having to deal with the situation. In Dawns mind they were both grown adults, there was no reason why they couldn't raise a baby, millions of people did it every day, how hard could it be? But inside she knew differently, having a Glimmer-Leon child was going to be anything but 'normal'; it was unheard of. The two groups didn't mix no matter mate. Glimmers work to restore and nurture for the better, Leon's play people like pieces on a chess board, working each pawn to the bone then scrapping them when a new game begins. Leon's live in sin, promote depravity and commit crime, their communities thrive in deprived areas feeding off of the weak and needy.

One similarity is that it is something you are born into, but unlike Glimmer it is something you are aware of as you grow up. Your whole world is centred around the core principles, if you know what to look for you can spot a Leon child grade school, they are the kids that don't like to socialise at recess, struggle to make friends and are often involved in incidents that no one can prove. Looking back Dawn could pick them out in her class photo, sadness surrounded them, a forced smile masking the darkness within them; she never really noticed them until now. A rush of panic pitted in her stomach, an unnerving flurry of anxiety infested her thoughts, her baby would be half Leon, her baby would be that kid. If Devin finds out about the baby he will want it to grow up a Leon, following his blood line and heritage. The anxiety morphed into a tight knot jolting her to the ground.

'He must not find out' she said repeating the words over and over clutching her small bump to protect it from harm.

Dawn needed to end it with Devin before he found out about the baby, maybe he wouldn't notice, maybe he wouldn't put two and two together. She paused momentarily deep in thought contemplating the choices that lay before her until one word left her lips,

'Angelo'.

*   *   *   *

She wasn't sure what she was going to say when she got there, she hadn't thought that far ahead. Dawn tucked her hands into her sweater sleeves to shield them from the cold air, strangely, she had never been to Angelo's house, they had always met at her Mom's or at the diner. It didn't take long to walk there, and the journey was quite pleasant allowing her time to think through how she would approach him with her unusual proposition. Dawn stopped outside the gate to his house, like Dawn he still lived at home, whether it was through choice or necessity Angelo's parents adored him being there. His Glimmer was passed through a split Vine, this meant that his parents were not actual Glimmers themselves, they understood the gift and probably had siblings and cousins who were Glimmer but they were not blessed with the ability. Walking through the rusty metal gate she felt a pair of eyes staring at her from the upstairs window, she didn't catch the person directly but she could see the red velvet curtains still adjusting back from their original position. He knew she was coming. The porch had a Texan vibe to it with old whitewashed planks creaking underfoot and two soft wicker chairs placed carefully in front of the window. Dawn reached to ring the doorbell but Angelo was already at the door, his soft eyes and cute smile still greeted her even in these difficult circumstances.

'Hey' said Dawn reaching her fist forward playfully to punch his shoulder,

'Hey' he replied avoiding direct eye contact.

The night air had changed from cool to cold, Angelo's warm breath clouding his path as he huffed towards the porch step,

'So, I know this is difficult, but I need your help….and you are the only one that I can ask'. Dawn said spluttering the next few words that left her mouth.

'I don't know what to do, I've got no one else to turn to…I need you Angelo, I need your help…please' she begged

'Please...if not for me for my baby',

An abundance of tears stained her face as she waited helplessly for a response. Angelo turned away dismissive of the dramatic show.

'What can I do Dawn, what can I do?' the words pushed forcefully through his teeth as he peered either side of himself to check for prying eyes.

'You got yourself into this, you never listen, you never think of anyone else, you're a liability to your Vine and they should know that'

'No' shouted Dawn,

'If anyone finds out then he will find out then I will lose her' she snarled like a lioness protecting her cub.

'What do you mean?' said Angelo

'A child of Leon blood should be raised a Leon, not Glimmer, he'll take her and insist she is brought up in his shadow and I can't let that happen Angelo, I just can't…'

The night fell silent as Angelo processed Dawns last statement; she dried her eyes with the sleeve of her sweater pushing mascara down the side of her face. Angelo's voice broke the silence.

'What would I need to do?',

'Something that I can never repay, but if you agree, it must be forever, I need your word, once it is done it cannot be taken back'

Dawn switched suddenly from emotionally unstable to deadly serious. Angelo grasped Dawns hand without a second thought,

'I'll   do   it'.

CHAPTER 14

RAEGAN

Weekends were lonely in her world, just two people sitting down to eat had never seemed enough. As a child Raegan imagined a full house, the buzz of lots of people crashing into each other in the quest for the first piece of pot roast. At most, there was four of them if her Gran and Alice attended but even then, the room felt empty. Raegan had been trying to contact Alice all day; she had called and texted her but had received no meaningful response. She imagined Alice sat chained to her parents dining table answering probing questions about her grades, extra-credit reports and social life or maybe they had eloped for the weekend enforcing their no cell phone policy both to avoid their own work lives but also to ensure Alice actually communicated with them.

'Hey sweetie' said her Dad as he carefully laid out two places at the table.

'You okay? you seem a little off with me today, are you still mad I didn't call you back last week, if so in my defence the cell signal was awful...'

Raegan could barely hear him over the heavy guitar riff surging through her ear drums.

'Rae… Rae' he said more forcefully the second time,

'Did you hear me? I said I'm sorry about last week, can we move on?'. I've brought dessert!' Raegan's ears pricked up at the last word.

'Frozen vanilla and berry yogurt, its already out of the freezer so should be at perfect eating temperature after supper'.

Her Dad wasn't a lot of things, but he was very thoughtful. Raegan called Alice again, hopeful that she would pick up and save her from a weekend of ultimate boredom. It went straight to answer machine.

'Damn' she cursed.

Although her Gran had classified her as a Mapper, Raegan had always felt like a Watcher, looking at the world through a thin glass window, never quite in the mix or participating, just watching from the outside. Raegan had promised her Gran she would stay away from over-crowded places to avoid tuning into any flickers that couldn't be controlled, just until she had learnt the discipline, and her Gran was positive she could learn. Raegan had readily agreed to her request as she certainly didn't want to face all those judgemental and uppity Glimmers again. The boredom she felt on the inside was physically represented by the speckled rain drops that scattered the front window; Raegan had transgressed so far into boredom she found herself counting them. After reaching near fifty-five she stuffed her head in-between her arms and watched the world go by. At this distance it was safe for her to watch the people and the thick insulted glass window also helped separate her from the chaos that her Gran feared. She watched numerous bright coloured umbrellas clash, drains fill and then be emptied by cars rushing by, small enthusiastic children were being reprimanded by their parents for daring to step one toe into the overfilling puddles. Lifting her gaze from events directly outside the house she looked through the street into the deserted public park to find a pair of crisp blue eyes staring directly back at her. In any normal situation this would be terrifying, but Raegan became energised, she sat up sharply clearing the moist air from the cold glass with her palm to ensure she was seeing correctly. He didn't move, he was rooted to the ground like a heavy crystal figurine that only she could see, people appeared to walk through him. He made one small movement of his hand gesturing Raegan towards him; her body twitched in response committing to the deed before her mind could catch up. She moved swiftly towards the door, she could hear her Dad rustling the cutlery ready to serve dinner, in her mind she was already half way down the street but her body stayed still, feet glued to the ground, she needed to decide, now or never. With one sweep of her jacket she chose now.

Raegan could barely hear the distant calls of her Dad over her heart thumping in her chest, she was flying as she cruised down the boulevard clutching her jacket over her head to protect herself from the pelting rain. At the end of the street she stopped to catch her breath, her pulse fluttering inside her stomach as the adrenaline started to subside. For a moment she forgot he was there, she was lost in her own private world contemplating the consequences of her impulsive decision. She could sense the frantic phone call her Dad would be making to her Gran and hear the disappointed tone in her voice.

'Hey' said Dom in a very aloof and casual way,

'You are over thinking this, they'll be fine' he continued,

'And why do you presume to know what I am thinking? This is your fault' she replied sharply snapping back to reality,

'It's not only Glimmers who have an inner sight you know',

His torso was wet through, jolting a small burst of excitement in Raegan, she stepped towards him assessing his soaked figure from head to toe,

'What did you say?'

'You heard me, you think you're the only one with a gift, well you're not'.

His words were strong, but his demeanour had dwindled, Raegan couldn't read him but sensed his anguish, pain and loss.

'Come on' he gestured, his hand encroaching forward into her space,

'I wanna show you something',

'We've been here before and it didn't end well' she said gazing back towards her Dads house contemplating her retreat.

'Come on'

Dom's smouldering eyes compelled her into following. Curiosity overcame her and she grasped his hand, the electricity was instantaneous and haemorrhaged through her body. She felt powerful, fearless, she felt secure.

The rain continued to beat vigorously to the ground, giant raindrops splashed on Raegan as Dom led her through the streets, both sets of hands clasped together intertwined so tight that the blood pooled in the tips of her fingers. The grey skies made this side of town darker than usual; Raegan was anxious about entering the area after her previous encounter. She pulled back, slowing his pace.

'Come on, we only have a slim window to get there' Dom urged. Raegan couldn't reply, she stood frozen, breathless,

'Hey' Dom gripped her hand drawing her in closer, she could feel the heat from his palm radiate through her body,

'Its fine, we're fine'.

Rain trickled steadily from his brow, Raegan took a deep breath and lunged forward across the desolate street onto the brick clad alleyway peppered with thick neon lettering on the walls. A few feet from the entrance stood a cobbled staircase enshrouded in shadow, Dom pulled a key from his back pocket and forced it into the lock. A thick damp smell hit her as the door slid open, it wasn't unpleasant, just intense. At first glance the place looked unliveable, there was minimal furniture, just a moth-eaten couch and a small wooden set of table and chairs. The bathroom off of the main room was cramped with a constantly dripping tap hitting the stone tiles. Raegan moved cautiously into the main room, taking in every detail.

'It's not much, but its home' said Dom,

His keys hit the small glass bowl on top of the old box TV in a ritualistic fashion. Raegan remained silent as she shuffled around in the small space, the whole place must have only been as big as her Grans lounge, it wasn't the dowdy furniture or dim lighting that shocked her, it was the lack of personalisation. There wasn't one picture on the wall or magnet on the refrigerator, in reality there was no evidence of Dom anywhere, this could be anybody's place and that made her feel uneasy. Dom sloped onto the small armchair exhaling his worries and concerns away, Raegan was still standing still her feet stuck to the shabby floor tiles.

'You can sit down' Dom said gesturing towards the couch,

'Thanks' she replied edging her way slowly towards the unappealing seat. The silence between them was deafening, the exhilaration of the chase had long dissolved and it dawned on her that realistically they were just two strangers sat in a rundown apartment. The hum of the artificial lights filled the void in the room and prompted the first real statement of the afternoon,

'These lights are like the ones in school' she said

'Yes, they hum a bit but the bulbs last forever',

She could not believe they were talking about bulbs, she had to stop herself from making any more mundane comments. Dom continued to rattle on about the different aspects of his apartment, but Raegan wasn't listening, she simply nodded along to the words coming out of his mouth. Her mind was somewhere else; she was transfixed on his face. It was so symmetrical, she remembered an article she had read once that had theorized that the most beautiful people in the world had symmetrical faces, apparently it is something to do with the brain finding symmetry natural appealing and based on her inability to take her eyes off of him it was definitely something Raegan found appealing.

'Are you even listening to me?' Raegan was stunned out of her trance by his questioning tone,

'Yeah, yeah' she shook her head of the unsavoury thoughts.

'Do you want something to drink?' Dom asked manoeuvring his way to the kitchen that was masquerading as a cupboard,

'Yeah sure', she replied trying to sound aloof and cool.

Dom opened the large white refrigerator and pulled out two diet soda bottles, from what she could see he wouldn't be offering dinner. Raegan apprehensively scooted across the sofa as Dom moved to sit directly beside her, the silence was just heating up when he turned his torso to face her.

'We both know the stories, we've heard the fables, but I want you to tell me Rae, I feel something' he paused just long enough to make her heart skip three beats,

'I think it's a good thing, but if I've learnt anything from those stories it is to be aware of who and what you are dealing with'

His sentence ended with a long gulp of soda; Raegan mirrored him using the time to think about her reply.

'Ok   stranger,   but   you   go   first'.

CHAPTER 15

DAWN

It seemed like the only logical answer, but something about it didn't sit right with Dawn. Sat at her overloaded desk she pondered other possibilities, wished for things to be different, it wasn't that she didn't like Angelo, but she still loved Devin. She could feel him outside the building, he came every day and waited for her, she tried to ignore it, but the feeling was deep in her stomach. Angelo knew he was there, he had set up a guard to watch the building during work hours, he escorted her to and from work, like a child being taken to school. Dawn was helpless, in all of the craziness she had lost control her Glimmer. The baby was disrupting her beacon. Her head was constantly fuzzy, filled with semi-full flickers from anyone she had contact with, she couldn't shift them or help them, they just sat stagnant on her mind, a constant reminder of how she had failed. Coffee was off the menu in her current state, so a tepid green tea perched on the edge of her desk, the smell turned her stomach but

Angelo insisted it was good for the baby, so she indulged him putting her disgust to one side twice a day.

Work had slowed down recently; Dawn didn't like to surmise but she had a suspicion that Devin had something to do with it. What most normal people didn't realise was that Leon's held significant power in their communities, a dark force was easy to spread and weak people were easy to manipulate. Tigar-Barton had slimmed down so much already, it was only Dawn left in the administration team and she didn't think she would be needed much longer. The office was a lonely place to be with no co-workers to talk to, she was sure the only reason she was kept on was because she was the first to start, and they didn't know she was pregnant. She couldn't tell them yet; it wouldn't be long till she would have to though. Her stomach had grown significantly in the last three weeks, her pants button was now being held together with a safety pin, it would only be days before she would need to start wearing maternity clothing. Dawn did not relish this idea, she had always been proud of her slim figure, wearing tight neat clothing was her normal and now she would be restricted to unflattering dresses and baggy pants. The green tea still sat on the desk, the unappealing liquid making her reflection look withered, Dawn stood up and walked the tea cup over to the office plant, she wasn't definite but the plant had taken a sickly turn since she had been watering it with green tea twice a day, and that was proof enough for her that she shouldn't be drinking it. The phone bleeped, breaking Dawns dangerous train of thought, it bleeped again, she prepared her most welcoming voice,

'Good afternoon, welcome to Tigar Barton, how can I assist you today?',

There was no response.

'Hello, can I help you', she repeated,

'Dawn' said the raspy voice,

'Dawn don't do this'.

Dawn was crippled, she had managed to stay level headed so far because she hadn't had any contact.

'Dawn, you don't have to do this' the voice repeated 'I love you'.

Dawn couldn't construct any words, she froze, clasping the phone with both hands, her ear pressed tightly to the receiver. She knew what she had to say but the words didn't surface, she crouched on the floor, phone still firmly in her hands to protect it.

'Dawn, I know you're there, Dawn please'.

'I can't do this' Dawn replied, and she slammed the phone down and pushed it away. In all the panic Dawn had barely taken a breath, she felt lightheaded. Whilst she pulled herself up to standing and the phone beeped again, this time there was no pleasantry.

'Dawn, I swear if you do this, I will have no choice but to find you, this won't end well', he said through clenched teeth,

'I will always find you Dawn; we have a connection me and you...' he taunted,

'He won't do it for you, he can't, it will never be real, we are real, me and you, remember'.

Dawns eyes filled with tears, she knew he was right, she knew it was the truth.

'I'm not doing this for you or me Devin, I'm doing it for her' broken sobs separated her words. Devin's tone changed, there was no more anger or pleading, just a deadpan vow,

'I will find her Dawn; you can't stop me'.

The   line   went   dead.

CHAPTER 16

RAEGAN

'I don't know what you have been told but we are not all bad' said Dom shuffling his feet nervously and staring directly at the tiled floor.

'I didn't choose this life, it chose me, I was born into this world and unlike you I didn't have the freedom of my childhood, this has been my world since day one' he paused trying to recollect a happy thought.

'My mother had seven children, six boys and one girl and she loved every single one of us, no one could take that away from her, but seven was too many and four of us got farmed off to other houses, it wasn't far away, just close enough to watch the remaining three enjoy my mother. At night I used to sneak back to a broken doorway and watch her read them stories and tuck them into bed'

Raegan reached her hand over to comfort him, but he pulled away, obviously hurting from the memory.

'We are not ranked like you' he said begrudgingly through his teeth,

'We are not gifted, if anything I would call it a curse, we search out the weakest and most vulnerable in society and we feed off them. Encouraging them to spend more, crave more and drink heavier to satisfy desires that should never be quenched. We are driven to abuse and sabotage people, we are the devil that sits on your shoulder, coerces your dignity and rational thought then spits you out and leaves you to rot'.

Rae sat calm, silent and shocked by his disclosure.

'Being Leon has not always been as cut throat; at times over the years I have heard stories of enlightenment and sophistication, where the leaders or Banes as we call them led us to be better people',

'Isn't that still the case now?' Raegan interrupted

'No, everything changed just after I was born, the current Bane was cursed by a devastating trauma, something so vile it changed him forever. He decided that if his soul could never rest then neither could anyone else's'

'So, you're bound to him?' said Raegan,

'Yes, and he can see everything'

Raegan sat upright looking anxiously around the room for hidden cameras,

'Not like that' Dom sniggered under his breath,

'Oh'

Raegan's cheeks turned pale pink with embarrassment.

'Can he see me now?' she said

'Ah, good question'

Dom jumped out of his seat excitedly ready to answer,

'This is a vacuum' he said waving his hand around the room puzzling Raegan with his gestures.

'A vacuum?',

'Yes' It's a space that is invisible to the Bane hierarchy, physically it is here, we are sitting in it but they cannot see we are here, hence why I wanted you to shift your butt in the street earlier'.

Raegan pondered for a second,

'Cool, so this place messes with space and time, a bit like a black hole' she said

'You were listening in AP physics' said Dom, a smug smile growing across his face.

'But why would you want to be hidden? Surely it's a lonely place to be?'

'Well that is the downside but without it you wouldn't be here with me'

Raegan caught a flash of genuineness in his eyes. It lasted only moments before it was broken by the sound of heavy footsteps outside.

'Hide!' said Dom as he disposed of the second soda bottle.

'Hide?' Raegan questioned scanning the room for a suitable place,

'Quick, in the kitchen cupboard' he said pushing her into the room,

'Really?' said Raegan half expecting him to reassess the idea.

'Yes, sense my urgency'.

Raegan climbed into the cramped space hoping there wouldn't be anything else alive in there with her. A small hole in the knotted wood allowed her squinted eyes to see what was going on. To be fair to the guy the most prominent smell in the cupboard was bleach and she had expected much worse. Moments later two heavily build men entered the flat wearing Khaki pants and black ribbed vest tops, they looked like two characters from a navy seal advert. Raegan peaked anxiously through the hole trying to keep her breathing under control, the last thing she needed was for this situation to bring on a Flicker.

'Devin is looking for you' said the shorter of the two men pushing his finger directly into Dom's chest.

'Me? Why?' Dom replied keeping his distance from the guy.

'There have been rumours circulating that you have a new friend' sniggered the second man pacing behind Dom acting like he was part of the national guard.

'And Devin believes these rumours? Anyone could have started them, loads of people have a thing about me, they would all like to see me go down' said Dom lifting his chin to assert his authority,

'Yes, but Devin has you on his radar, being first born Leon means you could have stature' said the short man emphasising the word 'could' as much as possible.

'Understood' Dom replied,

'I hope these rumours disperse soon Mr Carter; it would be a shame to waste such potential' said the taller man said slurping from the remaining soda bottle.

The two men exited the flat as quickly as they had entered, leaving the door ajar to make a point. Dom promptly moved to the cupboard to help Raegan out.

'That was close' she said, a bead of sweat rolling from her brow.

'A bit too close' he agreed.

'What was that all about, why can't you see me?'

Raegan had so many questions she wanted answers to.

'It's complicated' he replied edging his body another inch towards her.

'Glimmers exist to neutralise Leon's, but Leon's don't want to be neutralised',

'Don't you want to be neutralised?' the words teased embarrassingly from her mouth,

'That's a different story'

He moved another inch forward,

'It all went wrong when Devin got involved with a Glimmer and it ended badly, really badly, he played with fire and got burnt'.

Raegan took a step backwards breaking the chemistry between them,

'A Glimmer wouldn't do that' she said,

'Well she did, she led him on, then disappeared off the face of the earth, broke his heart. Rumour has it she killed herself and the family moved away a few years ago but his search has been fruitless, he's been looking for years'.

Raegan's eyes glazed over, puzzle pieces slowly merging together.

'There was also talk of a child, although no one ever knew for sure, but if legends are true and there was a child of both Leon and Glimmer decent it would harvest enormous power and influence…pretty cool huh' he said casually opening the fridge to grab another soda.

'Want one?'

Raegan couldn't answer, she felt like she had been punched in the stomach, her mother had killed herself…

'Can you take me home please' she said robotically,

'Sure, you ok? You look sort of pale; you're not going to faint again are you? he said,

'No, I just have some things I need to sort out'

CHAPTER 17

DAWN

Her stomach was swollen now, her skin stretched to breaking point with a medley of limbs wriggling constantly just below her ribcage. Dawn sighed, exhaling loudly to ensure her discomfort was public knowledge. She still wasn't sure how she got here, it had been a long six months, she thought her life would have been easier after she had entrusted herself with Angelo, but it hadn't. It became a daily battle to avoid detection; luckily Dawn didn't start to show until she was about six months pregnant so she managed to keep her secret from her employer until then, unfortunately Angelo felt a need to escort her to and from work. Dawn knew that he secretly enjoyed the control, she was sure Angelo always had a soft spot for her so this situation, no matter how twisted, had played right into his hands. As well as being kept captive by her own kin, her footing as a Glimmer had been compromised because of her misconduct with her consort, relationships between consorts were not forbidden but were frowned upon and as far as the rest of the world knew this was Angelo's baby. He had changed too, he had changed the moment Dawn had asked for his help, he felt betrayed, she had hurt him deeper than any break-up, you wouldn't know to look at him but she knew, she could see it in his eyes, he didn't look at her anymore, he looked through her.

Dawn was hot all the time and the feeble breeze created by the air conditioning was not helping her cause. She had spent days staring at the same four walls chewing on ice chips and wishing her baby out. She found everybody and everything irritating. The door creaked as her Mom entered,

'Beautiful day outside, the sun is shining' Dawn could feel the words scolding her newly found agoraphobia.

'Fish are jumping, and the cotton is high' her Mom sung in tune trying to lighten the mood. Dawn didn't find it amusing.

The day progressed like any other, watching re-runs of Friends and ER and eating everything in sight, she never thought she would hear herself say it, but she missed being at work. She spent hours picturing her baby, thinking about its tiny hands, its creases, its soft button nose, she didn't have a name yet. She needed to see it first, feel it in her arms and look into its eyes. A Glimmer name is more symbolic than other names, it needed to express light and virtue, not just be a name that they carried through life but a name that would carry them. Dawn felt a twinge in her side; heartburn, something she wouldn't miss. As Dawn slowly drifted off into her afternoon nap, something she had become quite accustomed to, the front door burst open. Angelo stood in the doorway clearly rattled,

'Dawn, Dawn' he startled her from her slumber,

'What's wrong?' she asked waddling slowly towards him. They were the words she had been trying to avoid at all costs,

'He's   coming'.

CHAPTER 18

RAEGAN

The night time air hit Raegan splashing waves over her body, she could barely remember the path she took to get home, in her original journey she had taken flight with Dom leading her steadily by the hand. Tears were cutting against her pale skin, more unanswered questions thumped through her mind as she darted through the park back to her side of the city. There was no comfort when she returned, she felt like an alien in her own environment. As she approached home, she stopped to look through the same window she was peering longingly out of earlier. Her dad was sat in his antique chair; the room was eerily dark with just a warm beam of light gleaming from his reading lamp. He looked apprehensive, his legs and arms contorted staring deep into space. Raegan paused and contemplated her next move, this could change everything, this would change everything. Moving closer to the door she felt her heart hammering inside her chest, she wished that her words would bamboozle and perplex him and that he would have a logical explanation for all of her erratic thoughts. The door flew open before she could even put the key into the lock, no words were exchanged as her Dad flung his arms around her squeezing the breath from her body.

'I'm ok' said Raegan reassuringly, but his grip did not subside, if anything he pulled her in closer like he knew what the next chapter was going to bring, holding on for a final moment before their world would change forever. Moments later their embrace was interrupted by a welcome voice.

'We need to talk to you Rae' said her Gran signalling her to the living area.

Several minutes past before anyone spoke, Raegan retreated to uncomfortable fidgeting, building herself up to the biggest question of her life. She wished Alice was with her, she was great at breaking tension with a silly remarks or inappropriate jokes. The silence ended abruptly,

'She asked me to do it Rae, she pleaded, I couldn't refuse her' blurted her Dad weeping into his hands, his heavy breathing accentuating his pain.

'It wasn't a choice, you have to understand, she had to do it'.

'There is always a choice' said Raegan, her voice breaking with emotion,

'There really wasn't sweetie, trust me', he said reaching his hands towards her to bridge the gap.

'Trust you?' Raegan moved swiftly away from his gesture,

'How can I trust you when you have lied to me my whole life, you told me she ran away, you told me she had to do it to keep me safe, not that she killed herself.' she turned to face her Gran standing by the panoramic window.

'It wasn't all a lie Rae, we wanted to protect you, we had to protect you, we made a promise'. Raegan started to sob uncontrollably.

'A promise, a lie, whatever you call it was her choice'.

Her body was overwhelmed with heat as she took a step towards the window. She knew what was coming but she was powerless to stop it, a surge of electric energy passed through her vulnerable body consuming her as her head tried to make sense of the words she was hearing. Unlike before, the energy didn't confine itself to her body, she could feel it radiating through the tips of her fingers and the soles of her feet. The ground beneath the three of them began to jerk unnaturally as Raegan struggled to control herself. Her feet, once solid to the ground moved erratically as her Dad and Gran grabbed sideboards for safety. A flood of images gushed through her mind; a crisp montage of events that had led to this moment. The most prevalent being Dom, seventeen years of memories and he was the reoccurring figure. Raegan brooded over this fact as she attempted to regain control, items once of value smashed onto the wooden floor, a fine mist of glass and porcelain filling the room.

'Rae' her Gran shouted,

'You need to release it…',

'Release what?' said Raegan shaking unnervingly,

'Release your fear' her Gran screamed through the deafening noise.

A bubbling rage filled her gut, a dormant volcano suddenly ready to erupt, she glanced at her Dad who sat anxiously on the floor clutching her Gran, like two small children awaiting punishment. She stared deep into his eyes longing for her Mother, she longed for her touch, her voice and she longed for answers to all her questions. In one rapid movement Raegan turned her body towards the large window and in an explosion of sound it cracked and broke into thousands of mosaic pieces shattering to the ground.

The house now stood deadly still with only the faint weeping of Raegan to break it. Her Dad and Gran rushed over to her body covered in the mound of glass and dust.

'I just wanted to know her' she sobbed, tears falling from her cheeks onto the shards of glass.

As her tears fell, a beam of late evening sun filled the room reflecting on the shattered fragments making a perfectly formed rainbow.

'I think she is closer than you think' comforted her Gran staring in amazement at the spectacle of light before them.

CHAPTER 19

DAWN

Time had never seemed so significant, only moments ago she was wishing it would go faster, now every second counted. Dawn stood paralysed in the centre of the room watching the disarray of possessions get shoved into black bags. The nursery had transgressed from an impeccable spectacle to a shabby mess, baby grows and diapers hanging out of draws, soothers scattered on the floor. Dawn had finished the room a few weeks earlier, she had decided on a neutral colour scheme with a cute teddy motif. She stood looking into the room that held so much potential, so many memories that wouldn't be made here. A single tear fell onto her blushed cheek,

'I'll only give you one' she muttered through her teeth,

'Only one'.

The moment of solace was cut short by her Moms incessant yelling,

'Come on Dawn, if you don't take it now, I might not be able to get it to you, you know he'll be watching every move I make'

The reality of the situation was finally hitting home, Dawn was leaving this place and she would never be able to return, she was having to disown her life, her family, her Vine, all because of him. It wasn't fair. Rage began to build up in her chest, it felt hot, frenzied and unpredictable.

'Dawn!' her Mom shouted from the hall, the ball of rage finally exploding,

'What?' she screeched,

'Ok, let us all calm down, we don't want everyone getting stressed out, it's not good...' but before Angelo couldn't finish his sentence Dawn interrupted,

'Not good for the baby, yes we know' her sarcastic tone stunning both of them.

The awkward silence was broken by the loud repetitive ringing of the house phone. Dawn's Mom answered it pre-empting what would be on the other end of the line.

'You have to move dear, the Bane are marching'. Dawn could hear the fear in her mother's voice.

'Get downstairs and into the car, we will just have to take what we have' Angelo insisted.

Dawn shuffled her way unsteadily towards the door, when she turned back suddenly making her way to the nursery, she plucked a small knitted bear from the floor and squeezed it into her handbag. As she exited the building, she could hear commotion coming down the street, the noise was brutal, similar to a baseball game emptying after a heavy defeat. The Bane were close.

'Come on!' Angelo urged as Dawn got into the old rusty Corvette in a very inelegant way. There was no time for goodbyes, Dawn barely embraced her mother as Angelo started the car.

'I love you darling' her Mom mouthed through the cold glass,

'I love you too' Dawn gestured back.

The engine roared as Angelo pulled out of the bay, Dawn could barely see through all her tears. As they pulled away, she could see Devin in the distance pacing towards the car, she turned and placed her hand on the back window, this wasn't how it was supposed to be. She could hear the faint sound of Devin screaming her name, but it was muffled by her relentless sobbing. This wasn't how it was supposed   to   be.

CHAPTER 20

RAEGAN

It had been a few days since the fallout, Raegan's life had gone quiet, even at school people seemed to be avoiding her, she dreaded to think of the rumours she had created. Before, eyes would look through her, except for Alice she could go an entire day without engaging with anyone. Now, not only did the eyes stare directly at her but she could feel their thoughts splattering onto the walls of the halls and rebounding straight towards her, each syllable etching into her brain; she wasn't sure how long she could take it. Home wasn't much of an improvement; her Dad and Gran were treading on eggshells around her for fear of another episode. Although her Dad hadn't mentioned it Raegan had seen the $1500 bill to replace the window. As the home room bell rang Raegan slowly collected up her things trying to delay the traffic of the hallways, as she placed the final book in her bag she stopped and stared at the empty seat three rows ahead. She hadn't seen or heard from Dom since she abandoned him earlier the previous week. At first, she wasn't concerned, she assumed he was busy, maybe slighting disconcerted by her hasty exit, but he wasn't at school, he hadn't turned up at her house and she couldn't feel him near.

Raegan carefully assessed her pathway through the hall scouting for specific targets to avoid before moving, turning the corner directly in her path was Alice, chatting idly to a red headed boy from her Math class. Raegan watched with a streak of jealousy as Alice gossiped happily without a care in the world, she wondered what she was so cheery about, was she talking about her? She watched for a final moment before promptly pulling her jacket hood over her head and starting to pace in the opposite direction. If she could keep her head down, she might make it to AP bio unscathed. Her strides weaved through the pubescent crowd avoiding chit chat and eye contact at all costs, she felt as if she was going against the flow, a single fish swimming upstream amongst the school. Eyes down she watched her feet take each step counting as she went to reassure her brain, she was making progress. The classroom door came into view through the pool of teenagers when a familiar hand jerked her to a stop.

'Hey Rae, I didn't realise you were in today, you didn't stop for me this morning' said Alice,

'Sorry, I was running late, crazy brain you know' Raegan replied still trying to make ground towards the classroom,

'Oh, ok' Alice paused sensing Raegan's reservation,

'I've got Bio' she announced politely gesturing towards the lab ahead,

'Sure, well I'll see you later then',

'Yep later'. Raegan swivelled back to her original direction, walking away she could sense Alice's unease and disappointment at their brief encounter, Alice didn't move from the spot until Raegan was fully out of sight. She didn't want to hurt Alice and that was exactly why it had to be like this. She wasn't going to hurt Alice.

CHAPTER 21

DAWN

The car bumped uncomfortably through the thick undergrowth, Dawn winced at every jolt and jostle; this wasn't an ideal route for a heavily pregnant woman. The day had been long and hot, the fluid pooling in her ankles had made them swell to twice their size and lose all normal bone definition. They were basically two huge water balloons at the end of her legs. The journey had been quiet with only a local station playing 1960's country covers on repeat. Angelo had engaged in minimal conversation making only basic statements about getting gas, eating and how far they had to go. Dawn couldn't resist asking every hour just to break the silence. Stretching her legs towards the glove compartment and making a sound of displeasure she turned towards Angelo like a whiny child,

'How long now?'.

With no idea where she was or where they were going it was the only way to get her bearings.

'We'll be there soon' he replied.

Dawn huffed blowing wisps of her hair from her face. The flat pack boxes that had been packed in a rush rattled in the trunk, she was unsure of how much of the stuff would make it to their new home undamaged. Peeking out of the highest box was the small teddy her Mom had knitted, it sat crooked and warped, one arm and leg trapped securely in the box, the other limbs bouncing unsettlingly. Dawn stared for several moments picturing what she had left behind, only now it was starting to hit her. She could not return… ever.

Her thoughts were briskly shaken away as Angelo slowed the car and began to signal left. By this point the sun has set with only a slim line of orange light breaking on the horizon. Dawn scanned the upcoming scenery, taking in minute details. Dirt tracks, dry broken ground, rough wispy grass; he was right, no one would find them here. As the car pulled up to the small dishevelled house Angelo took a deep soothing breath, he was relieved to have arrived. Dawn resisted the urge to make any ungrateful statements as she exited the car and began to inspect the building. The exterior lacked love and care and needed some solid time spent on it but only small ailments jumped out to her as she walked towards the large porch way. The air was humid in the dusky sun, Dawns skin felt sticky as she waddled up the front steps towards the curtained door. She peered through the tinged window, the house looked semi-liveable, furnished (although not really to her taste), it had potential she thought optimistically. Angelo lunged up the steps two at a time carrying a pile of boxes and bags as he came, he fished inside his front pocket and pulled out a rusty golden key.

'Here it is' he displayed publicly.

The door jolted open creaking continuously as it went, a rush of musty air surged towards them turning Dawns stomach enough to give her reflux.

'Needs a bit of an airing' Angelo said looking eagerly around the first room. 'Not sure if there is an air conditioning unit',

Dawns silent reaction to that statement was enough for Angelo to realise that it would need to be rectified.

CHAPTER 22

RAEGAN

Raegan was convinced most of her bio had been taught in another language today, even the English words didn't make any sense, she sat with her head on the desk peering over folded arms listening intently, learning about cell constructs just didn't seem important anymore. Raegan had always been an honour student and she had made numerous appearances on the honour roll over the last three years. School was never challenging to her, she didn't think she was overly intelligent, she just tended to understand things first time, but with all her recently acquired knowledge about her 'mapping' capabilities school had started to lose its edge.

The bell rang loudly in her ears signalling the start of recess, as before Raegan slowly packed away her things trying hard to avoid the bustling hallways. The lunch hall was a magnet for hungry teenagers, enticing them towards it with mouth-watering smells of hot pizza and fries. Raegan's lunch was not appetizing, a Dad special, tuna. She couldn't bear to eat in the lunch hall anymore, too many people made it difficult to concentrate, she tried her best to block it out but most of the time it was no good. She found solace in her secret space, well it was a secret until a few weeks ago when she collapsed in there, but time had played its part and the general population had forgotten its existence again. The room was convenient for Raegan but also rather inviting, its dilapidated state made it dark and cool, all things that helped her cope with the flickers. The air was dusty, the speckles magnified by a slither of sunlight that crept through the boarded window, the speckles danced hypnotically in the glow only disturbed by Raegan's small movements.

Sixty minutes can seem like a long time when you are by yourself, she sat on the broken chair, hood up with her headphones in, music used to be something that relaxed her now it was a necessity to block out any unwanted Flickers. She sat bobbing her head to the slow reggae sound trying to visualise a happier time, she pictured her mother in the photos at her Grans house smiling kindly at her from behind the frame, she thought about her Dad standing at the kitchen counter meticulously compressing his filter coffee and Alice walking by her side joking about her 'psychic Sally' abilities. Raegan longed for those simpler times, a small tear formed in the corner of her eye, poised to trickle down her pale cheek but before it could do such injustice, she wiped it clear.

'Not now' she muttered to herself.

As lunch break passed, she watched numerous shadows come and go under the door, drifting past on their way to next period. Curiously, two shadows stopped dead in front of the door and hovered there. Alice? She thought reflecting on their meeting earlier in the day, rewinding it in her head and cringing at her actions. The shadows remained fixed as the hallway drew quiet, hushed voices only meters from her, she slowly stood upright and crept three footsteps to the left to obscure the view. After a few seconds Raegan realised she was holding her breath in apprehension, the doorknob rattled momentarily before opening to reveal two tenth grade boys, they were slightly shabby looking, both with dark jeans and sweatshirts, Raegan didn't know them but did recognise them from around town. One had spiky hair the other dark and curly. They stood central in the doorway looking keenly around, they didn't look lost or like they were looking for a place to play hooky, they were searching for something or someone. Raegan felt vulnerable hiding in the shadows.

'You looking for something?' she said boldly moving out from behind the pillar, the boys looked surprised by the sudden introduction,

'Might be' said the short spiky haired one with a confident whip in his words.

'This place isn't usually very popular'

Raegan took a step forward securing her dominance, the two boys looked knowingly at each other and took a step forward in her direction.

'We know who you are' said the dark curly haired one flicking his curls back arrogantly,

'Or should we say what you are' his sidekick followed up.

Raegan started to feel her heart beat faster inside her chest, the adrenaline making her mapping hyper-sensitive. Within seconds a surge of flickers hit her like a rogue wave. She tried to barricade them in, but the boys started to laugh as her struggle became physically visible.

'He must be wrong about this one Dex' said the spikey haired one looking at Raegan with merciless eyes,

'Don't question Cam, just do it!'.

'Do what?' Raegan thought picking up fragments of their conversation, but before she had time to piece the fragments together a small figure glided in from behind her, nimble and unnoticed pulling a black cotton sack over her head. Raegan lunged forward trying to thrash herself free but was greeted by an ensemble of hands pushing her to the floor.

'This can't be happening' she reasoned with herself, this is a school not a young offender prison. Still pursuing her freedom Raegan kicked and squirmed several times trying to scream for help.

The two boys were obviously new to this as they scrambled on top of each other to try to secure her to the floor, one sat prominently on the back of her legs to reduce the violent kicks, Raegan was no soccer player but she could drop kick like the best of them. After a few moments she relaxed, held in a cross position by the three students, physical fighting wasn't going to get her out of this, she was outnumbered, she needed to be more cunning, think outside of the box and catch her breath. The hood they had placed forcefully over her head disturbed her at first; taking away most of her senses, but after a while she realised that it was actually helping her control and manage the Flickers, piece by piece a plan was coming together.

The room had become calm with only hushed voices breaking the silence, from the fractured sentences that she could make out the trio were in disagreement about something. Her only visual on them was through a threadbare patch in the sack, two pairs of worn leather boots, both scuffed from over wear. The boots were unmistakable; she had seen the same boots when she was hiding at Dom's place earlier in the week. Leons. Rae's mind raced as she placed the puzzle pieces together. How did they know who or where she was? Unease crept through her body, adrenaline kicked in and she began to shake, not with fear but with rage. She needed to create a distraction, it was almost physically impossible to fight off the three of them, together they were too strong. Staring at the green leather books that interrupted her view of the door she remembered the last time she was in the city, the man, the crates, the golden bubbles radiating out between broken shards of glass, the memory was painful but essential. Raegan closed her eyes tight and focused on the incoming flickers, if she could map into each one she could direct them towards her and use them to distract the Leon's. Raegan rummaged through the flickers in her mind, studying each one like a SAT question before deciding. Mrs Kane, the librarian was an interesting case; her flickers were tragic with the passing of her father earlier in the year. A pang of guilt hit Raegan as she felt her teacher's darkest pain, she didn't want to do this, but she had no choice. Her flicker showed a man in an apron baking large quantities of bread, he must have been a baker. Raegan pictured a young Mrs Kane opening a door to a warm room that emitted a syrupy smell, the room had an old wooden door and the young girl would peak through the knots in the wood to watch her father working his craft. The doorknob felt big in her small hands so required both to twist it open, her father would stand caked in flour to greet her, popping some of the misty powder on her nose and kissing it off. Raegan kept repeating the memory hoping she could pull Mrs Kane in. Minutes went by with nothing but continued confusion from the Leon's, Raegan was becoming tired of their indecision when another shadow appeared in the light beneath the door. The handle rattled viciously, and the trio began to panic, someone grabbed Raegan's foot and dragged her to the other side of the room, she continued to concentrate ignoring the frenzy surrounding her. The door flung open breaking the flicker, dazed and somewhat angry Mrs Kane eyeballed the three students standing to attention in front of her.

'What is going on?' she said, her teacher voice scaring the three Leon students,

'This room is out of bounds' she said as she looked hesitantly around the room for evidence of misconduct. In all of the confusion Raegan wriggled herself free, quickly removing the black cotton bag from her face and peering around the side of the desk, she wasn't going to be able to do this quietly, it was all or nothing. Just as the first Leon began to recite an elaborate tale about what they were doing in the disused classroom Raegan lunged forward dodging the three Leon's and clumsily barging Mrs Kane.

'Raegan Cole what are you…?'

But Raegan didn't hear the end of the sentence as she sped away, slipping and jutting on the polished floors. The hallway resembled an obstacle course; Raegan dodged students, ducked teachers and maneuvered through the maze, eventually making it to the school entrance. She stopped and turned briefly breathing in the place, she knew she wouldn't be returning to this part of her life anytime soon. The nostalgic pause gave way for the trio to catch up to her, Raegan's flight reaction kicked in and she bolted out of the large doors clattering down the steps, the contents of her backpack shaking furiously as she moved. The onset of rain had made her escape even more difficult; water ran down her face clouding her vision. She wasn't particularly athletic so the short burst of energy had already taken its toll, she tried to remember the words of her Phys Ed teacher, '*in through the nose and out through the mouth*'

Raegan focused on the words trying to get her body to react but soon it relapsed back to panic breaths.

In all the frenzy, Raegan had lost track of her route and found herself lost in a strange and lonely part of town. The rain kept falling heavy seeping through her hooded top and onto her burnt orange hair, this weather was not good for her curly hair, it either soaked up the rain and styled itself with long heavy locks or repelled it and doubled in size. The street was surprisingly empty for this time of day with only a few people taking shelter in shop porches waiting for the rain to subside, Raegan felt like she was the only person in the world as she paced rapidly down the sidewalk. As she glanced back to check her progress, she noticed the three Leon's at a distance behind her, they were walking now with a swag in their step; they knew something she didn't. Raegan continued at a steady pace towards her Grans house, her Dad would be at work so it would be the safest place to go, they couldn't reach her there.

The rain began to ease off clearing her vision, in the distance a tall hooded figure stood less than fifty meters from her, grounded to the tarmac. With his legs slightly parted and his hands firmly in his pockets he pulled the hood from his head and glared directly at Raegan, his dark eyes inspecting her from top to toe. He was both majestic and threatening at the same time. Raegan felt compelled to keep walking, her feet detached from her brain as it pleaded with her to stop. The rain had been replaced by a light mist that penetrated her sneakers, a squelching sound followed as she continued walking. Raegan squinted through the mist; shoppers had now started crowding the streets crossing between them so much so that she began to come to her senses. He was controlling her, he was pulling her in, he had taken all of the fear away, but it had all come crashing back as the connection was disrupted. Raegan scurried in between the shoppers trying to mix in and camouflage herself in the crowd but he could still see her, and he stood firm, body rigid, only his pupils twitching to the rhythm of her movements. Four more figures appeared in the alternative exits in the street like a pack of devoted wolves. There appeared to be no escape, the noise in the street heightened as an onslaught of flickers cascaded towards her; she needed to stay in control, but she could barely think straight. The noise soon drowned out any rational thoughts as her legs buckled beneath her, it was like the beginning except more intense, her heart racing as she tried to hold off the flickers. For a split second she surrendered, she wanted to let go, give in and stop fighting but a voice from deep within spurred her on, the voice was gentle but determined and strangely familiar. Within the montage of chaotic images an attractive woman leapt out to her, the voice muffled everything else going on, but Raegan managed to make out the words

'Use it, use it', the voice repeated over and over willing Raegan back to full consciousness. She knew the woman; they had met a long time ago; it was her Mother. Raegan placed both palms face down on the wet tarmac pushing herself up to standing, her demeanour had changed, confidence filled her body as she stared directly at the tall stranger. Taking three steps forward she focussed her mind to the shoppers, compartmentalising each flicker by simultaneously reading and mapping them one by one. To the naked eye the actions of each of the shoppers would seem strange as they bombarded the Leon's stalking the exits from the main street. Anything that could distract them would be enough, but Raegan saved the finale for the main participant. Looking around frantically she noticed the milk truck driving slowly down the cobbled street, bottles rattling and milk slushing from side to side. Focussing hard she established a connection with the driver and changed the direction of the truck. The truck sped up bouncing heavily towards them, but the tall man did not move, like a peacock ruffling its feathers he stood proud, Raegan willed the truck to go faster so she could escape but in all of the madness realised that if she wanted to do this, she needed to take control, she would not be the cause of another fatality. The truck began to slow and came to a gentle halt timed to perfection to skew the view of the tall stranger so she could slip away. He ran quickly to the front of the truck surveying the dazed crowd who were now moving back to their normal business, but she was gone, evaporated into the misty haze.

After the initial escape Raegan felt elation, running quickly towards her Grans apartment door checking nervously for anyone who might have followed her. She poised her finger ready to press the buzzer but hesitated, questions overloaded her mind, 'Who was he? She felt like a police interrogator booming questions at a suspect. Raegan sat curled up on the wet porch as the intensity of the day's proceedings slowly became reality. She sat quiet; expressionless and numb with one prominent image in her head, replaying over and over, her Mom was   alive.

CHAPTER 23

DAWN

Time had slowed at the new house, minutes felt like hours and hours felt like days. Only the tiny flutters of small limbs broke up the passage of time. Dawn sat deflated on the floral armchair, her bump protruding from her torso, her navel was now raised from her skin like an eject button that she did not want to press. The sun was hotter here, the air didn't flow like it did back home, it was stagnant. Not even a draft crept under the wooden door. Angelo hadn't got around to fixing the air conditioning unit, so Dawn's only solace was standing semi-naked by the refrigerator, this was not a favourable option, but it worked for her. Staring at the cluttered house you would think they had only just arrived, but emptying boxes was taking its toll on Dawn, even the nursery had lost excitement for her. Angelo was away most of the time only giving Dawn basic information about his whereabouts, she didn't question him, she had no right to after what she had done to him. After removing herself from the sweltering trance and finally opening the last box she heard a knock on the front door, not a feeble 'tap tap tap' from a neighbouring do-gooder bringing pie or moussaka to the new neighbours, it was an abrupt and purposeful 'Knock knock knock', the sort you expect to be followed by 'County Sheriff's office' but there were no such words that followed. Dawn looked apprehensively at the ABC clock hanging precariously on the wall. Angelo wouldn't be back yet, even if it was him, he had a key. The noise came again, this time slightly louder to assess whether anyone was home. Dawn peered carefully around the nursery door to see two shadows standing tall outside. From the size and stature of the shadows she assumed it was two men but why would they be calling at this time of day? Angelo never had anything delivered straight to the house. Dawn heard a faint mumbling as she cautiously tip-toed towards the entrance, the shadows then disappeared. Taking a long soothing breath Dawn stepped back against the torn wallpaper catching her bare foot on an upturned nail,

'Ouch' she cursed forcefully trying to keep the profanities to a minimum. As she bent down around her oversized stomach to inspect the damage the two shadows appeared at the side of the house peering in through the semi-coated windows. Dawn remained fixed, silent in the hallway trying her best to remain undetected although her sheer size made it very difficult. The two men scoured the building looking for any signs of life, making muffled statements to each other as they went. As they made their way to the back of the house Dawn heard the rumblings of a car engine pulling up front. Angelo paced up the porch steps carrying two brown paper bags,

'I'm home' he hollered, but from Dawns frozen expression he sensed he had walked into something suspicious. Dawn pointed urgently to the side windows miming wide eyed 'men at back'. Angelo's expression changed in the moment. He placed the two paper bags down and exited the house the way he had come in. Dawn was left with just sound to comfort her, she could hear Angelo making his way around the side, her ears following the creaking decked boards that circled the house, then nothing. Dawns legs started to throb in the awkward position she had got herself into, but she dare not move. Moments later Angelo emerged looking perplexed,

'No one there' he said holding Dawns gaze to comfort her.

'But I saw them, they banged on the door, they walked around the side of the house and looked through the window' she became irritated by his disbelief.

'I'm not crazy' she blurted as she walked towards the side window,

'I could hear them; I could hear them talking'

She looked expectantly into the distance. Her breathing quickened as she started to panic, eyes darting rapidly studying the long grass. Nothing. Angelo stepped back into the house and pulled Dawn close to his chest, he felt warm, comforting, she could smell the fusion of strong coffee and tobacco on his breath, this should have turned her stomach but it didn't. She fitted quite well into his embrace, even with a swollen stomach. Should this feel so good? she asked herself. Enjoying the moment Angelo rested his chin upon her head and breathed deeply, his chest pulling Dawn in closer as he inhaled,

'It will be ok' he whispered. As the words left his lips two small kicks impacted deep in her stomach, she felt an overwhelming sense of attachment. Maybe this could work.

'I will protect you' he said,

And for the first time since this ordeal began, she truly believed him.

CHAPTER 24

RAEGAN

Morning arrived quickly and with the adrenalin of the previous day Raegan had barely slept, her eyes broke open to embrace the morning sun, she felt calm and confident. The sepia pictures that scattered the walls greeted her differently this morning, gone were the melancholy memories, instead it was hope that was ignited in her eyes. Raegan stared deeply into the faded frame trying to connect the dots. She shifted her weight slowly in the covers to mobilise her throbbing limbs when her solitude was broken by a cough interjecting from the back of the room. Turning swiftly, she pulled the covers into a defensive stance. Sat on the rustic rocking chair in the corner was a young man, he was silent apart from the small repetitive throat noise he was making. Raegan retreated towards the door,

'Who are you? get out of my room!' said Raegan pulling a pillow up to cover her torso. The young man didn't quiver, his stance resembled a king on his throne, strong and stubborn.

'Didn't you hear me, I said get out' she said louder this time. He sat motionless, his eyes transfixed, Raegan refused to let her stare down first. A rush of bodies entered the room,

'Raegan what is all this noise? Are you ok?' said her Gran bumbling around her,

'Who is he and why is he sitting in my room?'

Her Gran glanced over in fake amazement,

'Oh James dear, what are you doing in here?' she said moving over to where he was sitting and pulling him to his feet, he was tall with a blonde quiff that cast a shadow over his right eye. He didn't speak, he simply glided from the chair to the door staring intensely at Raegan, his eyes so wide that the deep green colour oozed from them. Raegan's dad stood in the door as the strange boy left.

'We need to have a talk with you Rae, I think its best that you join us in the living room when you are ready'

He shut the door briskly behind him before she could question it. Raegan shook her head trying to work out if she had woken up this morning or whether this was an elaborate dream, why was everyone so calm about that strange boy being in her bedroom? It was creepy.

She felt violated and vulnerable, the madness of the morning had distracted her from her initial focus,

'They need to talk to me; I think it is the other way around' she said as she pulled on some suitable clothes.

The last time Raegan had been confronted by her family it hadn't ended well. As much as she fought against the idea, she knew she didn't have full control over her Glimmer, there was something inside her, a switch, that just snapped whenever it pleased. It wasn't a trait from her Grandmother so it must have descended from her Dad, although again he wasn't the type to snap, honestly, Raegan could barely remember him ever even raising his voice no matter snapping. Saying this, she was learning new and interesting information about her heritage daily, so she would have to put a pin in that thought for now.

Raegan walked through the warmly lit hallway into the living area, her Gran and Dad waited patiently muttering between themselves, she had never seen them this secretive. As she walked closer the muttering turned into polite and humorous chatter.

'Morning sweetie' said her Dad gesturing to the empty space on the seat beside him. Raegan smiled politely but chose to sit separately on the small cushioned stool.

'Just in case' she said attempting to lighten the mood.

The silence was deafening, each part of the parental responsibility waiting for the other to start.

'So, there was a strange boy in my room this morning…discuss' said Raegan, her sarcastic self-defence mechanism kicking in.

'Well dear, his name is James, he from Ellisville, two towns down, he's seventeen like you and he has just started attending Shaylock high, you'll probably share some classes together…' she paused gleefully,

'Right' Raegan replied feeling no more knowledgeable than the two minutes previous.

'He seems a nice boy Rae, genuine, strong, someone you can depend on' her Dad continued smiling uneasily at her Gran.

'This is all great information but what was he doing in my room this morning? and why is he suddenly part of our lives?' she said trying not to lose her cool.

'Is he some sort of long-lost cousin I didn't know about?'

She wanted the answer to be yes, he is an estranged cousin from the south who wanted to get some life experience, but deep down she knew it wasn't going to be that easy.

'Not a cousin, no Rae, although he is related to you in another way, you see James is part of our Vine' said her Gran glancing at her Dad for reassurance.

'After a Glimmer has appeared it is tradition to find a consort and although consorts do not need to be tied until they are twenty years old we thought because of your heightened gift that it might be a good idea to sort it out before then' she continued.

The room went silent for a moment, her Gran eager for her Dad to interject.

'That's basically it' he said slapping his hand on his thigh and bailing out of the conversation.

Raegan ran the last few minutes through her mind before responding; only one word seemed fitting.

'What?' followed by hundreds of others,

'What do you mean tradition?' 'Who thought it was a good idea?'. What the hell does it mean to be tied?' said Raegan dazed by the situation, her head was spinning as the barrage of questions spilled from her mouth, she was trying to keep her cool but she could feel heat thumping through her ribcage.

'Breath Rae, sit down' said her Gran, nervously paranoid about her own glass windows.

'What does all this mean?' she blurted out sharply this time, her Gran stammering trying to defuse the tension,

'It means James will be your wingman, your support, partner and maybe one day your saviour' said her Dad with fatherly rigor in his voice.

'So, I don't get a choice, it's all been arranged without me, what if I don't even like the guy? I don't need a babysitter'

'Well the higher Vine think you do, and they are not willing to negotiate either, it all out of our hands' her Gran said sternly.

Raegan collapsed back into the stool hunched tightly into a ball like a small child. Her life was slowly crumbling around her, decisions were being taken out of her control, she rejected the Vines decision, how did they know what was best for her? Raegan stood tall; her frustrations magnified.

'So, if this so-called consort is supposed to be all of those things, why didn't she have one?' Raegan pointed at the faded picture perched on the coffee table. 'Why didn't she have a saviour?'

Her Gran slumped ungracefully onto the chair staring tearfully out of the small window, Raegan waited patiently for the reply, but she didn't respond. The room fell silent before a defeated voice spoke out, his solemn voice capturing the attention of the entire room.

'She   did…it   was   me'

CHAPTER 25

DAWN

It had been four weeks since the two strangers had trespassed on the property, but she had seen nothing of them since. The days still felt long but she filled them with idle tasks, she had put together quite a routine based solely on her abilities to manoeuvre around the house. Her stomach could now be classified as gigantic, she never thought that skin could stretch so much, the bump protruded neatly and was barely covered by the meagre amount of clothes she owned. Most days were so humid she just let it all hang out, she had gone past caring and if she could grasp even five minutes of being comfortable every day, she would be content. Today the bump felt hard to the touch, the normally circular squishy bump had changed to an angled shape, she thought she might give birth to a UPS box! Angelo was out, he had been gone since sunrise, admittedly they were getting on better now, even with Dawns changeable moods but there was still a storm cloud above them ready to burst at any moment. Dawn had been uncomfortable for most of the morning; her back ached, her legs ached, and she had unrepentant heartburn still sizzling from last night's supper. Anyone would think she had eaten a full banquet with the intensity of her indigestion, not a poached egg. Slowly wiping down the kitchen surface she felt a sharp twinge in her lower abdomen, it made her wince, inhaling sharply as it peaked. It wasn't long before a second and third pain followed.

'Ouch' the fourth synchronised pain hit.

'It couldn't be'. Dawn glanced towards the calendar on the refrigerator door,

'Ouch' she winced again taking a deep breath to minimise the pain. Holding the kitchen counter tight the fifth pain radiated through her stomach followed by an almighty gush of clear liquid covering the floor,

'Crap' Dawn shouted waddling to the sitting area to locate her cell phone. Gritting her teeth through a mixture of rage and pain she fumbled through the cushions to locate her phone. Her moist fingers slipped over each number as she dialled Angelo, it went straight to answer phone.

'God damn it' she cursed positioning herself for the next contraction, they were getting stronger and closer together very quickly. The book said this part could go on for hours so why was it all happening so quickly? Dawn attempted to dial again. Engaged.

'Ahhhhh' she screamed collapsing forward onto the armchair. Her phone vibrated excitedly in her hand.

'Hey, what's up?' Angelo said totally ignorant to the situation unfolding,

'The baby is coming' Dawn shouted groaning through the pain.

'What now?'

'YES!'

The phone went dead; Angelo was on his way.

The next thirty minutes were agony. Dawn thought of her Mom, she was going to miss it, Dawn wanted to hold her hand and be comforted by her voice. She had barely been to any pre-natal appointments since they moved for fear of being seen. As the intensity and frequency of the pains increased Dawn hovered close to the ground, crouched on all fours she rocked side to side to ease the pressure on her pelvis. She couldn't focus on her cell phone so counted the gap between the contractions using Mississippi's. Her midwife was from the local hospital but that was over twenty miles away so Angelo would probably beat her here. Dawn pictured Devin, she couldn't help it, this was his child and she had taken away his right to be at the birth, the guilt was overwhelming and brought Dawn to tears.

'What have I done?' she said through her tears. Moments later Angelo ran through the door to find Dawn a blubbering mess on the floor,

'Hey, come on, we can do this' he said reassuringly, 'The midwife is on her way'.

After another contraction Angelo lifted Dawn and carried her onto the bed, he propped up some pillows and got the ice chips. Soon after the midwife appeared with a selection of vials and needles poised to take the pain away. Dawn had never been a fan of needles so politely rejected the offer. The pain had changed now, it was lower, more intense, guttural. Dawn could feel her body pushing and she panicked,

'I'm not ready yet' she said resisting the urge.

'It's time now Dawn, baby is ready to meet the world' replied the midwife calmly.

Dawn let the sensation take over, her body was now in control, she would surrender to it. Within minutes a small purple mass emerged followed by a gush of bloody mucus. The midwife lifted the baby directly onto Dawns chest. It was silent, not even a whimper escaped from its tiny lungs, Dawn rubbed her hands on its back trying to prompt it to breathe, slowly it turned from purple to pink and a small cry left the tiny human. It wriggled nervously on Dawns chest anxious in its new environment.

'It's a girl' Angelo stated in shock at what had just unfolded,

Dawn gazed down at the small bundle wriggling in her arms, she wondered whether all mothers were this terrified. Was her mother terrified when she was born? The elation of the moment subsided leaving her numb from the head down, her vision now skewed from a sudden downpour of hormonal tears. She cradled the baby's head awkwardly in her hands,

'A girl' repeated Dawn astounded,

'I will call her Raegan'.

CHAPTER 26

RAEGAN

Raegan had walked this path hundreds of times but never with this much pace. Her feet quickened beneath her as she got closer to her destination. Within seconds her finger was on the doorbell, she paused, composing herself before the confrontation. The door opened and Alice stood leaning on the splintered frame in a mismatched pyjamas and mauve sparkly boots combo.

'I need to talk to you, and I need you to listen to me' Raegan said placing her foot in the door well.

'I have been listening Rae, all I do is listen to you, you're the one who has been snubbing me, you have barely spoken to me in days, weeks even' replied Alice.

Raegan knew it was true, she had been so wrapped in her own world that she had forgotten about Alice.

'I am so sorry, I've just had a lot on my mind, I am an awful friend and you should definitely never to talk to me again after today'.

'Don't be dramatic, it's beneath you' Alice teased rolling her eyes at Raegan's suggestion. The girls stood silent on the porch, both waiting for each other to talk first,

'So, what do you need to talk to me about?' said Alice

Raegan didn't know where to start, or how much to tell her, the last thing she wanted was to tip her over the edge, Alice had an open mind, but Raegan's world was becoming more fantastical by the day.

'I saw the front of your house boarded up' Alice said stepping forward to console her,

'Yeah, that's part of the story'

Raegan shook her head towards the floor. The awkwardness was broken by the front door opening, Alice's Mom poked her head out.

'Hello Raegan, haven't seen you about for a while, everyone okay, how is your Gran?', she said

'Yes she's fine Mrs Kirkly, were all good', Raegan said politely.

She looked her daughter up and down.

'Are you getting dressed today Alice?',

'Yes actually, we are going out',

'We are?' said Raegan apprehensively,

'I don't know if that is a great idea...' her sentence was swiftly cut off by Alice

'We are going for a milkshake'.

'Lovely, good to get out on a nice day like this' Mrs Kirkly agreed retreating into the warmth of the house.

'I'll get dressed, you wait here' and Alice dashed back into the house. Raegan wasn't really in the mood for people, but she needed help, so she needed Alice.

*   *   *   *

The diner was as empty as usual, only a splatter of heads bobbed in the rundown booths. Raegan imagined this was once a vibrant place to go, the walls, once bright and colourful, were now faded and lifeless, the counter, once shiny and untainted now with a thick layer of grime that not even industrial bleach could get rid of. Raegan wondered how many stories lay in that grime; how many sad memories had been shared over a luke warm Latte, how many birthday celebrations had ended with spilt soda, how many young rebels had abused the scuffed red leather booths with graffiti when their parents weren't watching. She sat in the booth waiting for Alice to return to the table, she could smell the strong coffee brewing and it made her think of her Dad. She still hadn't fully processed the information she had received in the past few days; it just didn't seem real. Alice scooted into the booth with her complicated coffee and

Raegan's ice cream soda, the glass beaker was cold to the touch, Raegan's fingers poised on the top edge as she moved the glass to her mouth.

'So, how are you?' Alice said prompting Raegan to engage in conversation,

'Not good to be honest, I've got one hundred and one things going through my mind and not one of them makes sense' she replied.

'Ok, let's just start with an easy one',

'Well, yesterday morning I woke up with a strange boy in my bedroom'

Alice looked startled but intrigued.

'Yes, let's start there' she agreed,

Raegan opened up about everything, once she started it all gushed out. She told her about James, about her dad being her mom's consort, about her episode with the window and being attacked in the school by Leon's. Alice sat transfixed like she was binge watching a Netflix season, to be fair Raegan's story could be mistaken for an extravagant American drama.

'That is a lot of information to take in' said Alice nervously,

'Yep'

'How does Dom fit into all of this? Is he like your Leon seducer?'

'Alice' Raegan snapped,

'I don't mean it, don't be so touchy'.

Head in her hands Raegan's skin contorted as the gravity of the situation dawned on her.

'What are you going to do?', asked Alice

'What can I do? I feel lost, empty, my Glimmer is out and it is causing havoc everywhere I go'.

'Well at least Dom isn't around to make it all worse' said Alice sipping her cold coffee.

Her words took a moment to sink in, but they hit Raegan hard, she could feel her throat start to close as she played the words back.

'What do you mean Dom isn't around? where is he?'

Alice fumbled in her back pocket for her cell phone and searched the screen eagerly.

'Look, I had message sent to me from an unknown number, I assume now it is Dom'

Raegan squinted at the bright screen as she read 'HI, WON'T BE AROUND FOR A WHILE, TELL RAEGAN I'M SORRY',

'When did you receive this message?' asked Raegan,

'Two days ago'

'And you only tell me now, we have been sitting here for over two hours!' Raegan said with a raised voice.

'Keep it down Rae, I didn't think, you were in the flow', Raegan needed to stay calm, she needed to focus. Her skin started to tingle as she placed both hands on the freshly etched table, sweat leaked from her pores leaving a damp handprint in its wake.

'Are you ok Rae? What's going on?' said Alice confused by her sudden outburst

Raegan was paralyzed in her seat, she could hear, see and feel everything going on around her but she was unable to respond. Something had taken control of her, something dark. Alice was still speaking but she couldn't make out the words, they made no sense, she was cocooned inside herself petrified to move in case she caused the diner to collapse around her. She knew what had happened to Dom, they had him, he had him, and she was going to need to find out why. After a moment of clarity her calm returned instantaneously, as if it had never left; the diner was intact, Alice was not injured, and Raegan had taken control.

'We need to find him Alice' she blurted out,

'Where did you just go? You were in some sort of trance' questioned Alice

'I'm fine, I'm back now, we need to put a plan in place, we need to find him before they hurt him', she insisted.

'They? Who will hurt him? Raegan you are blowing this out of proportion, maybe he has transferred schools or is on a vacation.'

'He's not. I can feel it, are you going to help me?' said Raegan

'Of course I will, what do you mean you can feel it?' Alice was mystified by everything Raegan had just said.

'I will too' said a voice from the booth directly behind them,

James was sat bolt upright sipping a steaming expresso.

'When did you get here?' Raegan roared like she was talking to an annoying little brother,

'A while ago' he replied knocking back the second expresso.

'Aren't you going to introduce us?' he said pompously.

'Alice this is James; James this is Alice'.

Alice pronounced a half smile as she was unsure of how friendly to be based on Raegan's reaction.

'You don't need to be here; I don't need to babysitter' said Raegan zipping up her jacket and shifting in her seat ready to leave.

'I'm not a babysitter, I want to help, I'm supposed to help' he said feeling hurt by her coldness.

'I don't need your help' Raegan shouted as she started to walk towards the glass doors. This time she was loud enough to raise a few eyebrows from other customers.

'I know where he is' James stated bluntly as he lined up his two identical coffee cups besides each other. Raegan stopped in her tracks with Alice right beside her,

'Where?'

'I don't want to put you in undue danger Raegan, so I think it best not to tell you directly',

'Where?' she urged more forcefully this time,

'I can show you, but not here, follow me'. Her eyes locked on James searching for one truth in his words, would he help her? Was this a ploy to misdirect her? Raegan looked at Alice who seemed oblivious to her concerns.

'One more person can't hurt, can it?' said Alice shrugging her shoulders.

'Ok, but it's on my terms' agreed Raegan.

CHAPTER 27

DAWN

The books said the first six weeks were the worst; Dawn was in week eight and she had still not seen an improvement. She had read hundreds of baby books but none of them represented her baby. Carefully folded corners and brightly coloured post-it notes scattered each book; the thumbed pages had not offered any comfort. Dawn glanced at the neon clock, how was it only 8am. Babies didn't live in the same time realm as the rest of the world, they created their own miniature time realm and instead of having a calm beep sound, they cried and cried... and cried. Dawn looked down lovingly at the bundle wrapped head to toe dozing peacefully on the cotton sheets. It was these precious moments that made the other more regular moments disappear, as if by magic; all was forgotten, all was forgiven, they were the cleverest micro species on the planet, and they knew it. When Dawn opened her eyes again it was 10.15am, Raegan woke her with an almighty wail, she must have been fidgeting for a while, but Dawn had drifted off into a deep sleep.

Turning to acknowledge her daughters plight Angelo flew through the door lifting the baby from the comfort of her bed. He was a good Dad, she had made the right choice, if it could be classified as a choice at all.

'I'll change her' he said, voice hushed as he crept out of the dimly lit room, it might only be for a few minutes, but Dawn relished her time alone. She adored Raegan but being with her just reminded Dawn of everything she missed back home, her Mom, her Vine and Devin. She tried not to think about him, she tried to shut him out, but it was impossible when she had his eyes, deep aqua eyes that pulled you in. Dawn had tried with Angelo too, they had shared a couple of heart lifting moments but nothing else, not on her part anyway. She longed for the feelings to develop, for the butterflies to start, but they never came, it would have made the whole situation easier if they had. Staring at the circulating ceiling fan Dawn stretched her entire body to mobilise her muscles from their current slumber. After just eight weeks she didn't look too bad, her stomach had flattened back down just leaving pink slithers, a visual memory of birth imprinted on her body forever. The quiet was broken by a hungry wail in the next room,

'I think you'll have to take over in a few minutes Dawn, I think she's hungry' and based on the wet stain on Dawns T-shirt, he was right.

'Damn, ok I'm coming' she replied pulling her T-shirt over her head in haste,

'Did you hear me Dawn' Angelo said barging into the room, Dawn stood clutching her engorged breasts,

'Get out, I'll be with you in a minute' Dawn urged

Angelo quickly turned his back apologetically and left the room. Dawn stood for a second trying to absorb what had just happened, the awkwardness just kept spreading, how long could they go on like this? Reaching for a fresh T-shirt, Dawn heard Angelo bellow from the next room and sensing his tone she immediately ran towards him.

'You have a letter' he said pushing the brown envelope into her hand like it was burning through his skin, Dawn looked at the crumpled letter, it had obviously been on a journey to get here, its torn and stained appearance told a hearty story. The letter itself wasn't a worry, Dawn had received mail since moving to this house, but it had always been addressed to her pseudo name 'Heather'. This only had three words on the front of the envelope etched with an old worn biro, Miss D Hart, no address or zip code, just a name. Dawns long stare was broken by Raegan's whimpering cries. Lifting her eyes to meet Angelo's she said

'We've been found'.

*   *   *   *

It wasn't the season for rain but that didn't stop it pelting down onto the tiled roof, the sound echoed through the house but rarely drowned out the raised voices. To add to the layers of sound a small but powerful sob broke through trying desperately to get its mothers attention. His words repeated over and over; he claimed he wasn't blaming her, but his accusatory tone said otherwise.

'I just don't understand Dawn, after all of this time, how did he find us?'

Angelo paced the creaky floor in the kitchenette, the repeated sound composed the swansong to Dawn sadness,

'You must have been too careless Dawn, where are we going to go now?'.

Dawn couldn't answer him, to be honest, she wasn't really listening, her mind was engrossed by the envelope, her eyes tracing the letters of each word meticulously, not in fear but in fascination. On the surface Dawn knew what this meant, she could smell the toxicity of the packaging tape and bubble wrap, but deep down she felt a little relieved and a little amused by the whole ordeal, it meant that he was still looking for her, that she was still important. Raegan's sobbing turned into a full bout of screaming and Dawn raced to comfort her, even at this age her senses were top notch and she knew something was going on. She clung to Dawn as she was lifted from the small cot, her baby connected to her and calmed her down. In the adjacent room Dawn could hear multiple murmurings, Angelo was doing what he thought was best, she had asked for his help over a year ago and he would not allow anything to get in the way of that. Dawn was mesmerised by her daughter, she could spend hours just looking at her angelic face picturing their future together, first day at kindergarten, dance recitals, boyfriends she would bring home.

Dawn wanted to see all of it, she wanted every moment treasured, ten thousand polaroid pictures etched into her memory. Holding her daughter tight into her chest tears ran from her exhausted eyes, this couldn't be her life, this wouldn't be a life for Raegan.

CHAPTER 28

RAEGAN

The school library was closed on arrival, Raegan wasn't surprised, it was dark and it often closed soon after the last student left. The building looked different in the twilight, obscured by the shadows, it had an eerie quality to it. Raegan, Alice and James resembled spies lurking in the darkness waiting for the night guard to clock off, Alice peered around the edge of the brick patiently watching the middle-aged man pace in front of the main doors. Raegan glanced at her watch, 8.03pm, surely he would be gone soon. Five minutes later he was still pacing, Raegan was becoming inpatient,

'Can't we do something?' said Alice,

'Raegan can' said James promptly,

'What can I do?' she replied confused about his statement,

'You're a mapper, aren't you? You can make him leave',

Raegan mulled over the idea, she thought about the first time she did it, how much damage she caused, how she lost control and the consequences of it but her second attempt was more successful, it was the distance that would the main challenge this time.

'Raegan' James barked bringing her back from the trance,

'What?' she snapped trying to dismiss it.

'You can do this'.

Alice took a deep breath in anticipation of the upcoming events, like Raegan she saw the first time this happened, and it still plagued her. Raegan centred herself and leaned back against the cold dusty brick, Alice and James didn't realise but she had mapped before, the day she escaped capture from the rookie Leon's, but her body was trying to escape then, she did it in defence, she did it fleeing for her life. This was different, it was too quiet, she couldn't raise the energy, she closed her eyes tight trying to fixate on the guard's flicker. She pictured a vivid glow surrounding him and imagined herself drifting towards him, closer and closer, his flicker felt warm against her skin as she absorbed his energy. The connection happened instantaneously, and it sent a surge through Raegan's body,

'Have you connected Rae?' said a frustrated voice from behind her,

Raegan ignored him keeping her focus on the guard. He walked slowly to his left, talking discreetly into his radio, he picked up his black bag and walked away from the building.

'Wow Rae, did you do that?' Alice said intrigued,

'He realised he needed to get home to feed his cat' Raegan said with a slight snigger in her voice

'He doesn't even have a cat!'.

'Ok, feel clever do we? Can we get back to what we are focussing on'?

James's tone sobered the moment and added another layer to Raegan's loathing of him, she scowled in his direction to ensure he was aware of her distaste.

'Let's go then' said Alice urging the quarrelling pair to join her.

The trio promptly darted towards the school each of them checking to see if anyone was watching, as they approached the main doors Raegan took a sharp left and signalled James and Alice to follow her.

'Where are we going?' James said through gritted teeth,

'We can't just walk through the front door now can we, it will be locked and alarmed' replied Raegan

Alice nodded in agreement trying to catch her breath from the short sprint. The building was pitch black, Raegan skulked down the side staying close to the brick using her hand to feel for an opening, a few meters down the texture changed from rough to smooth as Raegan's hand traced the door. Crouching down she reached for the sharp object and shook it rigorously,

'Do you want to make any more noise?' said James from behind,

Raegan ignored the unhelpful comment and continued to rattle the handle.

'It's not going to magically open the more you shake it',

Raegan turned to meet James eye,

'Well what sort of plan do you have other than just standing there and watching' she said glancing towards Alice for an accompanying chuckle, James rolled his eyes and felt around his feet. Alice, who was somewhat oblivious to the tension building up between the pair, looked on confused by James actions, she stepped back to give him some space, wincing in pain she reached down to her ankle, she could feel the blood settle onto her fingertips. Alice picked up the sharp metal object and thrust it in James direction, she didn't want to be seen to be helping his cause but she knew Raegan would only continue her own plight to get the door open to spite James.

'Let me have a go' James announced.

Sliding towards the door he prodded the edges of the frame with the metal pole looking for a weaker area, Raegan looked over her shoulder to inspect the new plan, James wedged the pole into a moth eaten section and pulled the door from the frame. The door cracked loudly, it had obviously been secured from the inside to reduce the risk of intruders, splinters scattered the floor in front of the trio as the dust clouded their vision.

'We are in' said James, his voice laced with arrogance at his triumph.

Raegan ignored the comment and barged past into the dark corridor. The school looked very different at night; the lockers created large shadows on the floor that made the place feel very claustrophobic. The trio moved quickly towards the old library, the doors were locked, the metal lock laughing at them as they approached the entrance.

'Not again' Raegan said banging her forehead against the wood.

James flew in nipping something from the back of Alice's head, he peered into the rusty hole poking the hair pin in and rummaging it around. Raegan rolled her eyes disapprovingly, half of her wanted his plan to work but half of her wished him to fail. It wasn't a trait that Raegan valued in herself, but she couldn't help it, something deep down pulled the feeling out of her. The lock clicked and the doors edged open, the smell blasted them first, a mixture of antique wood and stale paper, the air was thick due to lack of ventilation during the day, it lay heavy on their lungs as they stepped thought the threshold. The task was going to be impossible, thousands of books sat static on the shelves, some hadn't been touched in years. Alice glanced at Raegan hoping for some for some sort of plan to unravel.

'Let's start looking in the directory for any books with key word in the titles, said Raegan. 'Vine, Glimmer, Leon, any hint of those, if that doesn't work then we will have to look ourselves'.

The prospect didn't enthral Alice, she had never been a fan of libraries, especially this creepy one, in the dark. The directory should have been digital by now but like many things at Shaylock high it was stuck in the past. The index itself was dusty and obviously hadn't been used in a while, some of the pages had fused together in protest at their lack of use. Raegan sifted through each page, cross referencing any keys words that came up, Alice doubled checked everything over her shoulder ensuring nothing was missed, she didn't want to be here any longer than needed. The directory didn't throw up any leads as to where to start their search, both girls were exhausted at the prospect of having to search manually,

'Where's James?' Raegan said peering through the rows of books, 'James?' she whispered loudly, there was no response, just her echo bouncing back.

'Where is he?' repeated Alice

A feint voice travelled through the thick air,

'Over here'

The muffled voice grew louder as the girls approached the dark corner of the room, James was knee high in books, speckles of dust twinkled from the ventilation hole in the roof, they surrounded him fantastically.

'Any luck with the index?' he said, knowing what the answer was going to be.

The book he was holding was leather bound with web scrolled up the spine, the pages were tinged mustard yellow and it smelt as bad.

'I think you need to look at this Raegan' said James pushing the book into her torso.

The words were tiny on the page and smudged in places, probably from the multiple leaks in the old roof over the years, but even through the defects Raegan could grasp the points on the page. The pages were set up like hieroglyphics, inked images dotted the page, the outlines soaked into the paper, the images depicted a story of two people, one with a light jagged edge surrounding them and the other inked in total darkness, the words underneath read like no others she had ever seen but somehow she could still read them. Raegan turned the page and instantly dropped the book, she stepped back gasping to get oxygen into her lungs, but they were closed. Alice caught her as she stumbled backwards over the redundant books,

'Rae, what is it? What's wrong?' said James,

She couldn't answer, she just glared at him, he mirrored her distorted expression letting out a long sigh.

'It says that the offspring of Leon and Glimmer are condemned to death, that they cannot survive with such polarised ancestry',

Raegan leaned against the bookshelf trying to piece together the puzzle. Raegan wasn't born of Glimmer and Leon, both her parents were Glimmers so none of this made sense, why was she being targeted? James clicked before she did, she saw the change in his eyes as the truth began to sink in. The enigma surrounding Raegan dispersed leaving an exposed shell of a girl standing defenceless by the desk. Angelo wasn't her Dad, not her paternal father anyway.

'This can't be happening' she mouthed grabbing the air to support her.

'It actually makes a lot of sense Raegan' James stated squarely.

There were still too many unanswered questions but the one she was most focused on was what Dom had to do with all of this. Was he sent to lure her in? Was he bait? Was he instructed to tell her that story about his Leon heritage? And most importantly, did he know?

'We still need to find Dom' she said, her agenda now twofold.

'He must hold the key to all of this, that's why they have taken him, we need to find him'

Alice started searching through the latter pages of the frayed book for any clue as to where he might be. James grasped Alice's hand stopping her in her pursuit.

'I   know   where   he   is'.

CHAPTER 29

DAWN

They had moved three times in the past two years, every time they settled, he found them. Angelo seems confident they would eventually out play him, but Dawn knew differently, she knew he would never let go. Leon's are persistent and predatory creatures, but they were also pack animals and they took care of their own. He would hunt Dawn down to the end of the earth to find Raegan. Dawn looked at her daughter everyday searching for her Leon side, but it never surfaced, she was relieved every time she hit a milestone and hadn't changed. Their current place of residence was a trailer in midtown of nowhere, the place was old, shabby, not somewhere Dawn wanted to raise an infant. Angelo had found it after three long days of sleeping in the car. Money was getting tight as he struggled to hold down a job, so it was harder to find appropriate accommodation. Angelo had been up all night on the phone, he hadn't bothered Dawn with any of it, he needed to feel like he had control when realistically he had none. Dawn sat bunched up on the top of the bed with Raegan cradled in her clammy arms, she slept soundly, even with all the fuss going on around her.

'Get some sleep' said Angelo 'We are moving in the morning'.

A mixture of relief and heartache hit Dawn, another move, another place, another start. She didn't reply, she simply obeyed and shifted her weight in the bed. She was beginning to lose her fight.

*   *   *   *

The car was packed to the brim, every time they moved, they had more stuff to take, Raegan's belonging were growing faster than she was; highchairs, walkers, pushchairs, all taking up precious space in the cramped vehicle.

'We need to stop for some formula' said Dawn as she plugged Raegan into her car seat.

Angelo sighed but agreed, they couldn't predict when the next gas station would have what they needed. The car pulled up alongside the pump and Dawn jumped out making her way across the sandy ground, it was getting hot already as the sun ripened in the sky. Glints of glass from smashed beer and soda bottles reflected brightly in her eyes, blinding her momentarily. The convenience store was on the side of the gas station, the bell rang as she entered, Dawn could see the CCTV camera following her every step, she pulled her hair over the face to skew the picture as much as possible. She swiftly moved over to the baby section scanning the shelves frantically for the formula. Dawn bent down reaching towards the tin to check it was the right one, her light dimmed by the ignorant stranger standing adjacent to her, she squinted to read the panel but then stood up to move away, as she turned two familiar faces stood blocking her way,

'Hey Dawn, long time no see' snarled Kane.

Hayes stood further back guarding the aisle so they wouldn't be disturbed. She wished she was hallucinating but she wasn't, they were real. She didn't cower, she didn't cry, she just waited silently.

'Long way from home aren't you Dawn, we've missed you' he continued.

Dawn didn't dignify his arrogance with an answer.

'Forgot your baby did you?' Hayes interjected thinking he was funny,

'Nah, it's with that coward consort of hers' said Kane,

'Bet she's a crap mother' Hayes continued talking through her.

Dawn moved swiftly towards him, simultaneously grabbing Hayes throat and pushing her knee into his groin.

'What did you say Leon?

The words forced through her teeth projecting small speckles of saliva onto his cheek. Kane laughed,

'Now is that anyway to greet an old friend',

'He's no friend of mine' Dawn seethed as she pushed her knee in further.

'Okay, okay' Hayes hissed through pained breaths.

'We're not here to hurt you or your little family' he choked. 'Devin just want you to know that he has you, he always has you'.

Dawn released her grip on Hayes, he stumbled back in discomfort. Kane held his gaze on Dawn as he skulked out of the store. The confrontation should have petrified her but instead she felt powerful. She pushed her hair back from her face and stood directly in front of the CCTV camera, her stare burning down the eye of the lens.

'You   want   me,   you   come   and   get   me'.

CHAPTER 30

RAEGAN

'You are crazy' were the three words Alice kept repeating over and over.

'It's impossible' was another comment. Raegan paced the room, backwards and forwards, her route becoming ingrained in the mouldy floor tiles. James had absconded to another part of the library and Alice was sat on the wooden desk scanning her phone for any useful information. The delay was hurting Raegan, she hated waiting for other people. The darkness that shrouded the room soothed her anxiety; glints of moonlight scattered across the room. Raegan heard James holler from the other side of the library, but she couldn't make out his words, she grabbed Alice by the arm and pulled her in his direction. Scouring the vast bookshelves Raegan moved closer to the corner of the room,

'This may be of some help' said James with a pleased tone.

Three connected computer screens sprayed a spectrum of neon blue images towards the girls.

'This is how we find him' he said confidently.

Raegan scanned the screens to make sense of what was in front of her.

'It is a blueprint' said James,

'Yes I can see that, thank you' she replied in her most grateful tone.

'What do you propose we do with it?'

'Use it to find where Devin is, thus finding Dom',

'Oh great, yes, let's go then…' she could no longer hide the sarcasm from her voice. 'Do you think it is as simple as strolling in and grabbing him? Are you that stupid?'

James huffed. 'No, but if you have another plan'

Raegan cut off the end of his sentence with her eyes, he felt it and stopped in his tracks. Staring at the blueprint made Raegan's eyes sore, all of the lines and colours blurring together like a riddle providing no clear answers. She stood back to get a full view of the drawing; Alice joined her hoping she could assist in some way. A small insignificant mark on the blue canvas jumped out to her, it looked like a small burn mark from a cigarette or candle, she peered in closer tracing her index finger along the lines as they fused together. A moment of clarity.

'I know what we can do' she said so quickly the words were almost inaudible.

James and Alice looked on intently, a quivering mixture of adrenaline and nerves.

'When I went to Dom's place he explained that he lived in a vacuum',

The other two pairs of eyes in the room glared at each other recounting the sentence they just heard,

'A vacuum like in space…anyway, that was why it was so awful, he liked living there because it was invisible to the Leon rankings and they didn't know about it, that was why he was able to sneak me in so easily' continued Raegan

'If we can get there then we are in, we can sort out the rest of the plan from there, they won't know we are there, and we will have the element of surprise'.

James and Alice stood silent, neither wanting to be the one who responded first,

'How do we know they aren't guarding it? How do we know if he is even there Rae?, this Devin doesn't seem a dumb person, he will work out what we are trying to do' said Alice.

Her response startled Raegan, she expected doubts and questions from James but not Alice.

'Well, if you don't believe in me then I will go it alone' her stubbornness a glowing beacon for-shadowing the room.

'That's not what Alice meant Rae, she's just protecting you' intercepted James

'Well I don't need protecting' she bit back.

Raegan pulled out her phone and took screen shots of the three computer monitors,

'You're either with me or you're not, either way, I'm going' and she strode towards the broken doors and into the night.

*   *   *   *

The wind had turned, its bitterness hit Raegan's cheeks as she walked through the backstreets. Alice and James followed on, their movements edgy and nervous. The streets were unusually empty, litter sprayed the ground catching their heels as they walked. Raegan knew the way, she had only walked this path once, but she could do with her eyes closed. The town changed quickly as they trio moved into Leon territory, the sidewalk started to dip with cracks and holes in the concrete, semi-lit neon lights flickered in the distance advertising a mix of gambling and liquor stores. Even the air changed, it felt dusty and dry as it went through their nostrils. Dom's place was only five minutes from their current location, they needed to blend in, Raegan and Alice pulled their hoods above their heads, Raegan glared at James as he lifted the collar of his jacket.

'Luckily, they don't know you' Raegan said rolling her eyes at his inadequate gesture.

As they turned the next corner Raegan noticed a bustle of people gathered in the street, they were stood static in the central avenue, a wave a chatter and whispers.

'We need to get over to that side' said Raegan,

The crowd stirred uneasily, shifting their steps like a pack of zombies,

'Did they hear you?' questioned Alice, peeking around to see if the pack had shuffled.

'If they did, that brings another level of difficulty to this problem' replied James.

Raegan wasn't taking any chances; she signalled her hand towards her mouth and closed her eyes. She focussed on clearing her mind, ridding it of all of the pain and upset of the last few days, the blueprint etched line by line into her memory allowing her to navigate visually through the crowd. She needed to divert them away from their path, Raegan had used her Glimmer on multiples before but only in the moment of crisis with Devin and there wasn't as many of them. Her Glimmer hadn't stretched that far before, she needed to map all of the pack simultaneously for at least twenty seconds so that they could slip through unseen, her mapping would need to be strong and believable. Raegan glanced to the dark sky for inspiration, the moon, a sitting crest in the sky, its light drifting down to the swollen streets. A moment of silence amongst gathered in Raegan's clustered mind,

'I   know   what   to   do'.

CHAPTER 31

DAWN

Moving every few months had been hard, she never settled in, made friends or got to know the town she was staying in. She had got used to her nomad life, given up on befriending other humans because having to make up elaborate reasons as to why you are leaving over and over had become tedious. Her favourite excuse was that Angelo was an important person in the American defence institute and he was being transferred, the less sensible one was that he was a Columbian drug lord who was on the run from the authorities; she would tailor her story to the listener.

Raegan was developing into a beautiful little girl, Dawn could hardly believe it had been 4 years, in some ways it had gone too fast. Dawn had been settled at the current house for five months now, Raegan had settled in well, as she grew up each move was starting to get harder to explain, she protested leaving the last house because of the bunnies in the yard. The bunnies would visit on cloudy days searching for food and Raegan had set up her own bunny restaurant on the back porch, at night she would sit and watch them creep up and steal the food she had left. She was such a caring little girl. The style of house Angelo found for them had never improved, as much as Dawn wished it would, he liked to find remote and isolated country houses so that he could set up his own perimeter of protection. On the plus side the new house was situated closer to town than any of the others so Dawn could walk with Raegan to the kindergarten and back every day. The kindergarten was great, it made Dawn feel normal twice a day. Dropping off and picking up her child like every other mother at the school. It also allowed Raegan to start making friends, make mud pies and paint gloriously colourful pictures that all merged into one brown mass in the middle. As much as it would have helped Raegan, the school knew nothing about her situation, Angelo wouldn't take the chance that someone in the school was Leon or knew other Leon's, he didn't trust anyone except himself and Dawn.

On sunny days when Angelo was working late, Dawn would scoop Raegan from school and hit the park for an ice cream, it wasn't much but it felt like a treat. After a few weeks another parent, Carol, started to join in with the ritual with her son Gabriel. Gabriel was a few months older than Raegan but the two shared an interest in wildlife and spent many hours digging in the soil for bugs, Dawn cursed after every dig as she tried to soak the dirt from beneath Raegan's nails in the tub. Carol also had only one child and travelled quite a journey to school herself, but she said it kept her fit and healthy and she was sure that most of the health problems Americans were facing today was due to them not walking enough, in her opinion it was too easy to jump on a bus or get in the car.

The last day they met at the park was a Wednesday, it was a typical bright and sunny day and Dawn had even lathered sunscreen on Raegan's forehead and shoulders to stop her getting burnt. The grass has become long and dry in the last few weeks and it was becoming difficult to see the children through the dense shrub.

'You going away this summer?' asked Carol,

'Nah probably not' Dawn replied with a sadness in her voice, 'Angelo is probably working; he doesn't get much time off nowadays'.

Dawn could barely remember her last summer vacation; it wasn't something her Mom did very often, but she did remember her last summer break before her life changed. She pondered on the three days she spent by the lake, it was only two hours from home, nowhere exotic but no less magical. The lake house was rented from a relative and Dawn had told her Mom she was meeting an old school friend for a reunion, it was obvious to her now that it was the lie that started all of this. Dawn wanted to look upon the time as horrid, she wanted to remember it as a bad decision and something that ruined the life she had, but she couldn't.

Every time she let the memory in she smiled from cheek to cheek, she could still feel the hot sun beating down on her toned body as she sunbathed by the lake watching him fool around in the fresh water. Her lips could still taste the bitter-sweet grapefruit they shared at breakfast, which she pretended to like just for him, she could picture the shooting stars that they watched cuddled up in a warm woolly blanket on the deck of the lake, counting each one and naming them childish names. Her head told her to hide this memory whilst her heart told her to treasure it and whilst most people would see her life as a tragedy, she didn't see it that way because out of all of the drama came Raegan. Her daydream was soon interrupted by the amplified silence of two small children, Dawn became aware of the silence before Carol did,

'Raegan' she called out, her eyes exploring the long grass in an ever-increasing manic state.

'Raegan where are you?' she called, her voice beginning to break in the panic.

'Gabriel' Carol hollered in a less subtle way,

'Shhhhhh' uttered a small voice from a few feet ahead, Dawn moved cautiously forward towards the sound,

'Shhhhhh Mom, you'll scare it' Raegan continued.

Dawns final step brought her to a small clearing in the grass where Raegan and Gabriel were squatted on the sandy ground, she didn't know what she was expecting to see, a dragonfly, a stick insect, at worst a dead field mouse, but not a snake. Dawn wasn't particularly scared of them, but she was scared of one being within three feet of her only child.

'Raegan, move away slowly' she insisted 'Don't make any sudden movements'.

'Mom it's fine, I've told him not to hurt me' Raegan replied with absolute clarity in her statement.

'I don't think snakes understand English Rae so maybe he didn't understand you properly' said Dawn trying not to show her anxiety.

Carol was not as patient with the situation and as soon as she saw the reptile, she screeched a succession of child friendly expletives and in doing so startled the once docile snake. The snake lunged forward towards Gabriel and nipped his right arm with his fangs. As the screaming continued the snake slithered away toward the shaded shrubbery. Dawn reached for her cell phone and dialled 911, Gabriel's arm became swollen and inflamed, Dawn tried to calm the now hysterical Carol so she could focus on the needs of her whimpering son. The emergency vehicle arrived within minutes bringing even more chaos to the once quite play area, in all of the commotion Raegan had slipped herself into the shadowed shrubbery in search of the disloyal snake, Dawn could see her but was unaware of what she was doing as she frantically tried to relay information about the event to the emergency team.

'Raegan come over here' she demanded trying to finish her conversation as quickly as possible,

'Raegan, I said come over here',

But Raegan just stood silent starting at a patch of parched ground. Her fists were clenched tightly and her body rigid with anger. Dawn walked closer,

'Raegan I've just said...' and she stopped abruptly as she processed the scene before her,

'He told me he wouldn't hurt me' Raegan said through muffled sobs

'He told me we would be safe...he lied' she continued turning her body towards Dawn for comfort. Dawn looked upon the scene in terror, had she done this? Had Raegan massacred this snake?

'I was angry at it so I told it to die, I told it in my head Mommy, I didn't touch it, I didn't mean to hurt it, I'm sorry' she cried weeping into Dawns cotton vest.

'No worries, hey' Dawn turned on her best soothing Mommy voice,

'These things happen, go over and sit with Gabriel and Mommy will take care of it'.

Raegan walked wilfully away from the bloody scene and Dawn glanced down at the distorted snake, the question she wanted to ask just wouldn't leave the tip of her tongue, it couldn't, not ever. She brushed the remains under the nearest bush and took a long deep breath. She hoped it would never come to this, she was hoped it had skipped a generation or her genes had been the stronger ones, but they hadn't.

Raegan was Leon.

CHAPTER 32

RAEGAN

It would take all of her energy to map the entire pack, so she needed another plan, Raegan knew she wasn't strong enough or experienced enough to pull it off, she needed to think in a simpler way. The plan was almost ready, just the final finishing touch to add, Raegan handed Alice her jacket.

'Are you sure about this?' Raegan said as she pulled the jacket around Alice's shoulders,

'Yes' said Alice for the fourth time in the past three minutes,

'James will be with me, won't he?'

'I can't Alice, I need to stay with Raegan, she is my consort' Raegan rolled her eyes, both touched by his sentiment but also annoyed.

'I don't need you to be with me, I need you to protect Alice, if you want to help me you need to protect her, if the plan works we will only be separated for a few minutes'

'If the plan works?' repeated Alice slightly louder than the previous statement.

Raegan blocked her reaction out.

'You need to go in that direction, draw them away from the Central Avenue, even just a few of them will give me a chance to get through' she said.

Raegan peeked around the corner, in expectation but all of the commotion in the square had cleared.

'Where have they all gone?' said Raegan,

James's eyes joined hers as they scoured for any signs of life.

'That's creepy' said James, a shiver ran down his spine.

It made no sense; they were just there.

'What if it's a trap?' said Alice under her breath.

It was quite possible, and Raegan knew it, she couldn't underestimate how much he could see, maybe he already knew they were there. Raegan turned to Alice,

'We'll stick to the plan'.

Alice nodded and disappeared into the square followed by James, he turned briefly making full eye contact with Raegan, she didn't need him to speak, she could tell what he was saying, maybe they had a deeper connection than she originally thought. Once alone, Raegan kept close the cold brick, pressing the nape of her neck flush with the wall, she hadn't noticed how cold it had become, she could see her warm breath combust with the night air, she slowed her breathing down so not to draw attention to where she was. A brief glance across the square and it was clear something was wrong, Alice hadn't signalled yet, Raegan took her cell from her pocket. No message. She looked again, curious as to their whereabouts. Nothing. The candle wasn't lit in Dom's flat; it was pitch black.

'Come on, come on' Raegan mumbled her patience running thin.

She took a final glance towards the window and there in all its glory was the small flickering tea light, to the average passer-by it was nothing of significance but to Raegan it meant they were both safe. Now she could venture to her plan, and it didn't involve putting people she cared for in danger.

$$* \qquad * \qquad * \qquad *$$

Alice and James sat huddled on the floor in front of the window staring bleakly at the fading tea light. It had been easy to get there, too easy. They had followed the plan to the millimetre but Raegan still hadn't appeared.

'Where is she?' said Alice through gritted teeth,

She peered carefully over the bottom window pane, no sign of her. James felt foolish, he has put too much trust into his new consort, deep down he knew she would stray.

'This is turning into a senseless game of cat and mouse' said Alice,

'It's not going to be easy to track her now' has she got her cell with her?' asked James,

Alice fumbled in the depths of her backpack.

'It's not here', she confirmed.

'Well that's positive, Alice open your cell and see if you can track her phone' said James

Alice turned the screen brightness down to avoid prying eyes, James continued to be on look out, this place was so cold, dreary but calm. His eyes moved across the grey cinder block walls; chunks of concrete were missing creating a soft whistle of wind in the small room. This was not the sort of place James was accustomed to, he had grown up in a very stable and warm place, with a family who loved and appreciated him, he imagined this existence only rendered pain, surely no human being could he happy here, but Raegan had been happy here, if only for a few moments, he could see it in her eyes when she talked about it. He wasn't jealous, that wasn't the emotion he was feeling, he was sad, because although he would be tied to Raegan, and he believed that was his true pathway, he knew he would never have the whole of her heart, he would always only be   her   consort.

CHAPTER 33

DAWN

It had taken fourteen hours to arrive at the place where this had all started. The drive was long, but it had given Dawn space to think, uninterrupted quiet, away from the bustle of her now lingering existence. The call had been short, she didn't know how he did it, she had been standing waiting for a cab after a late-night trip to the grocery store when the phone box in the adjacent street started ringing. It rang three times before Dawn picked it up, she should have known with the first ring that it was for her. Two words were spoken with a gruff and tainted tone 'Diner, Tuesday', then the phone went dead, he knew it was her and she knew it was him, that hadn't faded with time. The drive back made Dawns stomach churn; waves of nausea grew in intensity as she got closer to her destination. She opened the window to break her drowsiness, she didn't want to stop but a coffee would do her the world of good. She pulled into the next gas station and dimmed her lights, except for the teller the place was empty. She walked confidently through the ribbed plastic sheeting and straight to the coffee bar.

'One coffee to go please' said Dawn, urgency oozing in her words.

'Sure' replied the attendant, his large body rotating awkwardly behind the register.

'Cream?' he asked with his southern twang,

This must be quite the shift thought Dawn. The machine whirred loudly as the coffee slowly dripped into the cup, the smell was strong, this would keep her awake. In the back room the phone rang, Dawns ears pricked up and she glanced at her watch. 11.05pm. Too late for a managerial call, maybe a girlfriend she questioned scanning the teller whilst arguing against herself, the teller shuffled into the back room. Dawn was hypnotised by the trickling coffee, so much so she failed to hear what was being shouted from the back room.

'I think it's for you' he said.

Dawns breath was undercut by the words being processed by her brain; how could it be for her? The five steps it took to reach the phone felt vast, every step took a kilometre of energy, she pressed the receiver to her ear and listened intently

'Diner, five hours' and the line went dead.

Dawn hadn't realised how far Devin could stretch, he must have people planted all along her journey, he must be watching every step. She placed the receiver down and grabbed her coffee.

'Thanks' echoed in the shop as she raced back to the car. It wouldn't be long before Angelo would ring her to check-in, so she needed to make up some time. She squeezed the gas pedal towards the ground and screeched from the gas station, her coffee spilling on the top of the paper cup. She was awake now.

*   *   *   *

The journey was flawless, not a kink in the road. The car had cruised seamlessly the whole way. Dawn had plenty of time to think but her thoughts were cloudy, the closer she got to her destination the more she felt torn by what she should do and what she had to do. This wasn't a journey she had imagined making again, she had dreamed it, but the dreams always turned into nightmares. She could sense him miles before the diner, he was already there, he had probably been there for hours so that she would feel this way. The road ahead stayed clear, she had called Angelo from a phone booth fifty miles back, she couldn't tell him with words but he knew from her tone that something was wrong, she kept the conversation short, told him to take care of Raegan and keep moving, she would find them when the time was right. Angelo had not replied, he was more hurt from the risk of Dawn letting her guard down with Devin than her physical safety, he knew Devin wouldn't hurt her. He didn't have the balls. Angelo also knew that the chemistry between them was electric, well it used to be. Dawn glanced at the clock on the dashboard, she had been driving most of the night and the faintest glint of morning sun was starting to creep into the horizon, this used to be a comforting sight but recently it made her feel anxious.

The diner sat like a glowing ember in the desert, the world was still asleep with only a mere few rising to prepare the city for the new day. As Dawn drew closer the neon signs changed from blurry clouds to crystal clear words, the 'R' still with its flashing glitch that used to drive her mad. As she pulled up to the dusty car park she scoured for another Leon, but it was empty. Although her senses had not been in their optimum state recently, she was sure that they were the only two there. The light had changed from auburn orange to a yellow glow, the air felt homely and refreshing after years away in the central wilderness. It was like déjà vu. Dawn parked her car close to the entrance in case she needed a quick escape. The diner was deserted, as expected at 5.45am, even the drunks wouldn't be rousing yet. As she entered the room he was sitting with his back to the doorway in the middle booth, he had chosen it carefully, their names would still be etched into the mouldy wood under the table. A delinquent dream between the two of them surrounded in a heart shape that only they knew was there. A secret declaration of love inscribed forever. The place smelled the same, the coffee percolating slowly in the pot, he must have had someone set that up for him, he was not the domesticated type. The door swung shut behind her, he didn't flinch or move at all, his stillness was unnerving. Time slowed as she walked towards the booth, her breath radiated through her chest, she needed to stay in control.

'I didn't think you would come' said the familiar voice,

Dawn was speechless, she had spent months shouting at this man in her head but now she couldn't assemble a single syllable.

'I'm assuming you came alone' he continued, fidgeting with a lighter in his hand. 'I'm glad'.

Devin turned to face Dawn, his face drawn with a sadness ingrained in his eyes, how long had he been like this? The last time she saw him he was racing towards her car with pure rage in his eyes, that was not what she saw now, she saw a broken man.

'I figured as you went to so much effort to get your message to me, I should make the effort' she replied.

Devin forced a semi-smile in reply, Dawn broke eye contact and moved towards the coffee pot, it had been a long drive and she needed the pick me up.

'I thought you would be surrounded Devin, I wasn't expecting it to be so quiet',

'Ah, how things have changed' he sneered gesturing Dawn towards the table.

'I suppose you chose this table by mere coincidence?' Dawn questioned, Devin inhaled a deep breath,

'Look Dawn, I didn't bring you here to reminisce, I brought you here to give you an ultimatum'.

'You aren't even gonna ask about her? You're just going to jump in with your thing and pretend she doesn't even exist' said Dawn

'Well she doesn't exist to me does she', he replied his voice peaking uncomfortably.

'You made sure of that' he continued.

Dawn was taken back by the change in his voice, this wasn't anger it was pain. Her stomach fell in her gut; how different this could be.

'Anyway, that's in the past' he composed himself.

'I need you to do something for me' he said standing tall next to her.

She had forgotten how he towered over her, not in a threatening way but in a protective one, his body still strong and foreboding. Dawn stepped back putting space between them, she needed to keep her head switched on and not get drawn into his addictive aura.

'What was so important that you had to see me urgently?' asked Dawn,

She was highly aware of the time and wanted to get back as soon as possible. Devin stepped forward counteracting Dawns previous movement,

'I need you leave Dawn' he said looking down at his feet,

'What do you mean? I came here because you wanted me to and now you are asking me to leave?' she said forcefully, taking a step towards him.

'No, Dawn, I need you to leave, for good, I need you to disappear',

'What do you think I am trying to do Dev, I have been trying to disappear for months, but you keep tracking me down, just stop looking and we will be gone'.

Dawn was chasing her breath as she replied.

'No Dawn' Devin paused,

'I need *you* to disappear, I need you to be gone, vanished, dead.'

His words choked Dawn into a panic, her eyes darted around the diner looking for her assassin, her pulse rocketing, sending her Glimmer into chaos.

'Hey, I'm not going to kill you, that's not how this is going to play' said Devin trying to comfort her,

'You are going to do it and I'll tell you why you are going to do it' he took another step forward forcing himself into her personal space, the heat from his body diffused into hers.

'If you do not follow these orders, I will finish your Vine, I will take down each and every one, including that consort of yours'

Dawn was silent and jarred by the statement, she was stuck in her space, her body wanting to escape but her mind unable to move.

'And don't think I won't do it Dawn, because I will'

Devin backed down moving towards his seat to revisit his coffee leaving Dawn immobile.

'I can't leave her Devin, you can't make me do that' she said,

'You can, and you will' he replied, 'You have thirty days'.

There was no quiver in his voice, no love in his tone, if he ever had a soft side, she had surely killed it. Devin left the diner before Dawn could react to his request, her body numb with shock, the new day sunlight forcing itself onto her face through the grubby windows, the warmth once comforting now filled her with fear. She needed a plan; she couldn't let him win. She would not leave Raegan.

CHAPTER 34

RAEGAN

This part of town was new to her, and that was risky in itself. The buildings seemed taller, the shadows sharper, the streets lights radiated an urban yellow glow against the grey brick. Raegan hadn't planned much beyond ditching Alice and James; she couldn't be responsible for any more pain and to Devin they would just be collateral damage. She kept close to the sides of the street, avoiding eye contact with anyone, her hood pulled up over her head to blend in. She travelled north along the main street but the further she travelled the tighter the pathway became. Soon she was walking on a path no more than three feet wide, her head told her to turn back but something drew her further and further in. The street was isolated, only Raegan's brisk steps broke the silence. As she turned to follow the path the atmosphere changed, a bustle of laughter radiated from the window at the end of the street but it did not feel daunting or inject fear into her, she was pulled towards it. Her steps slowed as she crept towards the building, an array of voices tumbled out of the window, so muddled in their conversations they sounded foreign. Raegan crouched under the window trying to pick out Dom's voice, Was he in there? After a few minutes the raucous laughter settled and Raegan could pick out a voice, she knew it was him, not Dom but Devin. Her heart thumped in her chest prompting her hands to begin to tingle, she could see herself breathing creating clouds of vapour in the chilled air.

'How do you know it will work?' bellowed a gruff voice from the back of the room,

'You told her to disappear Dev, what did you think was going to happen?' continued another. Raegan pushed her hand over her mouth.

'Who are you to question me?' his voice paced,

Each individual syllable being pronounced perfectly, his voice did not sound like he had been raised as Leon, he did not have the established twang that the other members had, his words were polished.

'This isn't just about you though is it Dev, the outcome could affect all of us' spoke a quieter voice from just beyond the window.

Raegan could sense anger in the air, a black cloud descended over the window. Nobody spoke after that. Devin launched towards the outspoken man, chairs and tables flying through the air, a mixture of stale smoke and ale drifting out of the window towards her. She couldn't see what was going on, but she could feel her throat tighten as Devin held the small man against the wall.

'Without me, you are a nothing, remember that' he hissed into the man's ear,

Still he did not let go, the fading sounds of the man slowing choking to death froze Raegan, she could feel his pulse slow as the blood struggled to circulate his body, but then Devin released the man and he crumbled to the floor, barely breathing.

'Nobody touches him' commanded Devin,

'If he is to live, he must work for it'.

Devin moved closer to the open window; Raegan cowered beneath it not wanting to be seen. His eyes remained focused forward, towards the small window in the opposite building, a faint light twinkled.

'Someone get me Kane and Hayes; I think we are going to need to keep a close eye on our guest this evening'

He slammed the window shut, so hard that the glass shook and fractured in the corners. Raegan crawled past the window and made her way to the other side of the path, if she was to find Dom tonight, she was going to have to get to him before Kane and Hayes.

CHAPTER 35

DAWN

The journey home was long and interrupted by several mishaps, all, Dawn predicted, orchestrated by Devin to reinforce his point. Only thirty minutes after leaving the diner her tyre began to lose pressure, with some investigation it appeared that small nails had made their way into the middle segment – nothing Dawn couldn't fix. Two hours in and she was losing gas, on inspection a small hole has pierced the tank and unfortunately, she wouldn't be able to fix this alone. She pulled into a garage just off of the highway, she was suspicious about everybody, she had to be. She didn't trust Devin, maybe this was all part of his plan to make her *disappear*. She drove across the dusty ground directly in front of the mechanic.

'I have a hole in my gas tank, can you fix it?', the man turned, glanced at Dawn and turned back to what he was doing.

'Excuse me, I asked you a question', she said

'Yes and I heard you' he replied, 'But I did not hear any words of kindness to go with the question'.

Dawn was slightly startled by his accusation, so she opened the car door wide as a gesture of good will.

'Apologies, it has been a long night' she explained,

'If you can fit me in, Sir, can you fix the hole in my gas tank so I can get back to my little girl before bedtime, please'

'Well that's more like it'

The man rose from his knees and moved walked towards her. He was taller and younger than he had previously appeared. He moved his hand forward.

'My name is Maz, nice to meet you',

'I'm Dawn' she replied.

'Looks like this car may have more issues than just a gas leak' said Maz circling the car.

'Yeah I know, but that is all I need done to get me home'

'And where is home if I should be so bold?'

'About three hours south of here',

'You're a long way out then, must have been an important journey',

Dawn didn't reply, she had done her best to avoid thinking about it for the last few hours.

'Well its gonna take me about an hour so I suggest you make yourself comfortable in the diner across the way. They serve great pie.'

'Thank you' said Dawn, relieved that she would make it home before the day is over.

'Is there a phone?' she asked

'Yeah I think so; you'll will need a few dollars to get it working'.

Raegan handed Maz the keys, grabbed her bag and meandered across to the diner. The brown wood-clad building was a ruin of its previous self, lots of the exterior had rotted away leaving exposed bricks and wires, the door had one glass panel covered by cardboard. Dawn walked in and found a stool by the bar, the stools were usually for loners and that was what she wanted to be, she tried to avoid places like this; it was a Glimmers nightmare, too many sad faces and stories to count. Luckily, there was only a smattering of customers and they all were with other people. The waitress approached the counter,

'Coffee?', a question she must ask hundreds of times a week,

'Yeah sure' Dawn replied,

It couldn't hurt, she still had a long journey ahead. The coffee was thick in appearance, not really to her taste, but the smell was comforting, more than ever now. She wanted to get home, to get back to Raegan, to Angelo, as much as he pushed her buttons, he was always there for her. How was she going to tell him? She rested her head in between her hands, eyes focused on the thick brown liquid swirling in the cup. Time was passing too slowly, she glanced at her watch, only ten minutes had gone by, impatience saturated her body.

'Got somewhere to be?' interrupted a voice, Dawn glanced her eyes up,

'You could say that' she replied avoiding the question.

The waitress continued to dwell in Dawns space, her incessant gum chewing creating an uneasy ambience.

'You should be careful, if you continue to stir your coffee like that it might just disappear… Dawn', Dawn sat up startled.

'What did you say?' her words quivered from her mouth.

'Nothing Ma'am, that will be two dollars',

Dawn stared at the waitress, she realised she hadn't taken a breath, she robotically reached into her purse a chucked a handful of dollar bills onto the counter, she felt claustrophobic, they all knew. Dawn staggered to her feet, pulling her jacket and bag tight to her chest, everything was blurry, what was in that coffee? She launched towards the door and dashed over to her car.

'Is it done? she shouted,

'Yes, but the resin is just setting, you need to give it another 20 minutes' Maz replied

'I don't have 20 minutes' she yelled,

With that Dawn screeched away from the garage, dust clouds broadcasting her exit. She just prayed that the tank of gas would get her home. The whole journey had been a disaster but what did she expect.

*   *   *   *

Three hours later and she was home, back in the middle of nowhere but it was safest she had felt in a while. As she pulled up the sun was just setting over the grasslands, its beauty lost on the troubled Dawn. Raegan ran from the house clattering down the wooden steps towards the headlights swiftly followed by a bellowing Angelo.

'Raegan do not run up to a vehicle that is still in motion' he shouted

Dawn pulled the car to a halt and took a moment to take her all in, her short orange hair bouncing just beneath her chin, her piercing green eyes that could convince even Angelo to get her what she wanted. She had the unkempt appearance of a scruffy, well-played child.

'We weren't sure when you would be back, so we made spaghetti' said Angelo in his usual disapproving tone,

'We made the sauce from tomatoes we picked from garden' said Raegan,

'Well that is amazing baby girl, I can't wait to try it'.

Dawn took Raegan's small soft hand in hers, she wanted to hold onto this feeling, to take in every microbe of her because whatever happened she would not be able to be part of her life for much longer. Dawn glanced at Angelo, no words needed to be said, he knew everything.

After they had all finished their supper Dawn tucked Raegan into bed, she didn't want her to be part of the conversation she was going to have to have. She kissed her forehead, the saltiness of play lingering on her lips as she turned down the light. As the door clicked shut Dawns heart stammered, she had to see this as short term, if she didn't, she might as well just die. When Dawn re-entered the kitchen, Angelo had poured her a drink,

'I thought you could do with this'

'Thanks' she replied pouring the fiery liquid down her throat.

'How   are   we   going   to   do   this   then?

CHAPTER 36

RAEGAN

It had been twenty minutes since Raegan had left to find Dom, she was only guessing where he was, but it was all she had to go on. James and Alice would be worried about her by now, they have probably gone back to tell her Gran, she would be livid. The streets were kind to her, a little too kind, she made her way easily to where Dom was being held. The building itself had no security but it was vast, and it would take a while to search. Raegan made her way meticulously through each room with no avail, she kept climbing the numerous staircases in hope that he would be there. A faint murmur of whispers echoed on the staircase, Raegan listened intently to detect its direction, quickly climbing the steps that led to a separate section of the building, these steps were narrower and the brickwork began to deteriorate beneath her feet. She came to the first door and rattled the handle, it was locked. She continued up the steps to another door, the glass on the front window was damaged with graffiti that she couldn't decipher. The door was open. The volume of the whispers had increased so Raegan moved cautiously trying to shut the door without making a sound. As she stood back to hide in the shadows, she felt lost, she hadn't found him, she had failed on her quest. She crouched against the wall, her shoulders sinking in defeat, her plan would need a rethink.

'I can't believe you came' muttered a voice from a few feet away, Raegan was startled by the voice, she wasn't on her own.

'Dom?'

'You shouldn't have come, it's a trap' he said his voice shaking.

'I wasn't followed' Raegan replied.

Dom started sniggering under his breath,

'What's so funny?',

The sniggering increased to a full laugh as he folded into a delusional state. Raegan grew impatient throwing her weight towards his cowering body.

'You weren't followed, no, you were led, every step of the way', he said

'What do you mean?

The door flew open revealing two towering men, Raegan looked to Dom, but his head was down, defeated. A surge of Glimmer raced thought her veins, she tried to focus it on the men at the door, but she could not connect. They were impenetrable. A wicked laugh circulated the room, it came from Dom's direction but was too intense to be him.

'It's lovely to meet you Raegan, I've waited a long time for this moment' said Devin, his tone calm as he moved from the shadows.

His image was different up close, he was strong, not just in physicality but in persona, he loomed respect. Raegan had imagined a tattooed, tight t-shirted body builder from what she had been told, but he wasn't, he was dressed in trousers and a collared shirt, a trilby sat proudly on his brow with an auburn beard spattered across his chin. His most prominent feature was his eyes, she recognised them, she had always been told that she had her father's eyes and now she saw it, the piercing aqua blue looking straight through her, dissecting her like a lab rat. Raegan did not return the compliment; she did not reply at all.

'Not pleased to meet me then?' he probed further pacing steadily towards her. 'If only you knew the truth Raegan…Raegan is a very pretty name, the one good thing she did for you',

'Don't you dare mention her' she snapped.

'Alas she speaks!'

Devin brought his hands coolly to his torso, Raegan tried not to rise to the bait, she needed to stay in control. A flicker was coming, her emotions were acting as a catalyst, sparking numerous connections with the people around her.

'Oooh, you're getting good at controlling it Raegan, I'm very impressed' he taunted.

Raegan continued to ignore his goading, if this was going to work, she would need to be able to control everything. Devin gestured to the men by the door.

'Kane, sort it',

Kane marched confidently towards Raegan, passed her and grabbed Dom.

'He can go now; he is no longer needed'.

Dom crippled at this statement, pleading for Devin to change his mind.

'Actually, bring him to me'. Kane dragged him back towards Devin,

'Look at me boy', Devin commanded

Dom's eyes tilted to meet Devin's, no words were spoken, they didn't need to be, Devin had banished Dom from the Bane, he would never be welcome as a Leon again, he would lose his heritage, his family, and his future. Dom yelled as he was dragged through the door.

'You don't know what you have done Raegan, you don't know what you have done…' his shouts turned to whispers as he was led away.

Raegan stood stunned in the centre of the room.

'Now, this is our chance to get to know each other, no distractions', Raegan nodded nervously,

'On one condition' she said,

'And what might that be?

'You   tell   me   what   happened   to   her.'

CHAPTER 37

DAWN

The plan had been set, the pain had been felt, now it was time to get it done. If it was going to work then it had to be believable, if Raegan was going to be safe he had to believe she had done it. Only two people in the world would know the truth and Dawn would be totally dependent on them coming through for her. Her mother had not agreed lightly, but then again no mother would, but she knew the possibilities of the power that Raegan had and it could be truly terrifying if it was not managed, even more terrifying if it fell into the wrong hands.

The day started normally, Dawn walked Raegan to school along the dusty path adjacent to the highway, the two-mile walk took her little legs forty minutes and they were her favourite minutes of the day. The warm sun shone low in the sky, the light breeze infused with engine oil and lavender filled her nostrils. She never knew what game they would play, yesterday it was the cloud game, last week it was the car game and today Raegan had chosen to play 'my favourite things'. They spent forty minutes listing all their favourite things in the world. Raegan's were rainbows, ponies and oranges, she liked lazy mornings, hot days and her beautiful little girl, she always ended the game by saying that Raegan was her favourite and today was no different, except Dawn was sad when she said it, she had a quiver in her voice. Dawn wanted that journey to last forever, they walked slower this morning and she squeezed in as many words and kisses as she possibly could, it was so painful, it felt like her chest was going to implode. Before she left, Dawn reached into her pocket pulling out a small wooden necklace held on a thin metallic chain, placing it over Raegan's head she sung a short verse of words creating a beaming smile on the face of her young daughter.

'You keep this safe for me, you promise?' said Dawn holding back her own emotional reaction.

'I will Mommy, I won't let anyone touch it'

Raegan turned and ran towards the door, greeting her friends and modelling her new necklace as she went in. Instead of turning to make the long walk home Dawn waited at the gate until Raegan was out of sight, she even held back a few moments longer. The ache weighed her down on the journey home, when she arrived Angelo was waiting, he hadn't said much since they had decided on the plan, Dawn didn't think he knew what to say. This wasn't just breaking Dawns heart; it was breaking his too. He would be the one who had to live the lie for the rest of his life, to feel the pain every birthday and Christmas and mourn with their small child. He had given his life to Dawn once, he was going to have to do it again.

CHAPTER 38

JAMES

He only waited for another fifteen minutes before he suggested they go and get help. It wasn't ideal, he didn't want to get Raegan into trouble, but he didn't know what else to do. This was new to him, well, mostly new. Alice stayed close as they moved through the dark streets, her nerves blistered her clothes, James stayed focused, his Glimmer was roaring. He was a Steerer, he did not have the Glimmer of Raegan but in the short time they had been together his power had been amplified, his flickers were happening more frequently and were more intense. Alice hadn't initiated a flicker as yet and this was puzzling to him as they had spent several hours together over the past few days but James had felt no flickers from her, he wasn't disappointed but she remained a mystery. One of the benefits of having a Glimmer was that you could look into people's hearts and minds, this made it easier to approach people, especially girls.

James' Glimmer emerged when he was fifteen, it was summer break and he was staying at his Aunts. His Aunt lived forty minutes away, by a lake that James spent many a summers day. This particular day started as any other, James and his cousins suited up and walked the short journey to the lakeside, he could remember the day clearly as it was particularly hot, so hot that the hairs on his body stood to attention whenever a cool breeze whipped past. His cousins, Colin and John were both two years older than James, they were chiselled, strong and good looking, girls flocked to be with them, James did not have the same magnetism. He was viewed as the feeble one, the boy that hung around like a bad smell. He loved the lake, but he did not think much of the company. The day of his change was no different, whilst his cousins were entertaining by the shore, James had taken himself into the depths of the lake, it was cool on his sizzling skin. The fresh water was smooth, and his limbs cut through it with ease, so easily that he drifted. James lay on his back floating idly watching the sky slip past, his breath shallow. He first noticed a different in his navel, a burning sensation that made its way around the circumference of his body, a slow panic settled onto his face, had he been stung by an eel? Had he brushed through some poisonous plant life? Within seconds his body became paralysed and he had not managed to call out for help, gradually he sank, watching as the light dwindle above the surface. He couldn't breathe, his lungs beginning to ache as the carbon dioxide took hold, his body occupied by heat excreting small bubbles from his skin, the water directly surrounding him was literally boiling. James recalled the exact moment he accepted his death, he had descended almost ten meters and the water had grown dark, the sunlight could barely reach him now and he was moving into the end of his second minute without oxygen. He closed his eyes; in his head he did not want to be found hours later goggle-eyed. The heat he had been feeling had subsided and he grew cold, in true Hollywood style this was all happening in slow motion. James reached his hand to the surface to salute the life he was leaving when a small spark shot from his forefinger, his vision had become blurred from the lack of oxygen but he squinted to watch his other fingers follow suit. The sparks travelled down his arm and through his body, to the naked eye it would have looked like they were travelling through his circulatory system. The heat he had felt started to return as his arms and legs recovered their feeling. The water swirled around him pushing him to the surface, he thought he was dreaming, he thought he had slipped into unconsciousness and this was a muse to take him to his death; but it wasn't. The breath he took when he arose was the best breath of his life, his lungs inhaled urgently and passionately in an attempt to inflate, his eyes hurt as the glaring sun pierced through, beads of water pooled on his forehead and cheeks. He was alive. He felt different, but he couldn't clarify how, his mind was rushing from place to place trying to make sense of what had just happened, James settled and started to make his way to the shore, when he finally got there the place was deserted. No cousins, no girls, no awkward family picnics or dog walkers. He pulled himself to standing, his body heavy and caked in a mixture of sand and silt, he could not see anybody, yet he could hear a large cluster of people, all talking over each other at different decibels, a mixture of fear, love and anger coming through in their voices.

James' eyes explored the area around him, not a soul to be seen, the voices became deafening and confusing.

His primal urge to run took over and he ran at lightning speed back to his Aunt's house, time didn't make sense to him, the sun was still up but the street was deserted. James started to feel like he was drowning again, this time instead of water pulling him down it was voices. He closed his eyes tight and pulled his arms taut to his chest, his torso now soaked with sweat exuded warmth, he held his breath in a plea to quieten the voices but they continued to build up to a climax. Then nothing. Silence and darkness. It was dusk, the streetlamps illuminated the gloom. When James opened his eyes the world seemed translucent, he felt in control, he felt vibrant. He could hear everything and everyone, but it was not as overwhelming as it was only moments earlier.

'James' a familiar voice shouted from behind him, Colin stood at the end of the drive 'Where have you been? We nearly had the coastguard out searching for you'.

James didn't respond with words, just a hand gesture as he glanced back out to the lake. He couldn't rationalise what had happened to him that afternoon, but he knew whatever it was it was going to change his life forever.

'James' said Angelo breaking him out of his trance,

'Yeah' he replied,

'Where's Raegan?' he asked

James bowed his head in shame,

'I don't know'.

'What do you mean you don't know?' shouted Angelo 'You are supposed to stay with her, you are her consort, that is your job',

'I know, I know, she lied to us'.

Alice nodded in agreement supporting James' every word.

'We had a plan to find Dom, but she went off without us, you know what she's like' said James,

'Yes, I know she is a vulnerable and irrational young woman who is overwhelmed by everything going on in her life at the moment'. Angelo said livid at the young consort's poor choice.

'Calm down everybody, shouting at each other isn't going to help' said her Gran calmly,

I'll   call   the   Vine'.

CHAPTER 39

DAWN

They only had a few hours before Angelo would need to collect Raegan from school so they had to efficient and organised, definitely not words Dawn ever thought she would use to describe her own death. Dawn had stirred up several scenarios that had all been gratuitously turned down by Angelo; she wasn't sure what he wanted from the whole situation but after a long night of discussion they had finally agreed. They barely spoke the whole way there. What were you supposed to talk about in these situations? To be honest Dawn preferred the silence, she could control her emotions in silence, but it was uncomfortable, it had been uncomfortable for a while between them. This might be a good thing for Angelo, he could get on with his life, find love and happiness and everything you are supposed to find in your twenties. The heat was climbing in the car, so Dawn wound down the window, the warm breeze splashed her face, it reminded her of her trip to the lake. Her heart pumped a little faster as a barrage of memories confronted her, she always tried to push them back but sometimes they were just too strong, she needed to control her physical response to them or Angelo might catch on. She should hate Devin for making her do this, she should loathe every part of him, but she didn't, the forbidden fruit, the one you mustn't touch – it was always going to be Dawns downfall. She lay back in the seat and imagined the damp sand clinging to her shoulders as she tilted towards his body, his cool and gentle fingers caressing her neck. Dawn squeezed her eyes tight to block out the next part, she couldn't go there, she wouldn't let herself. Angelo glanced at his watch, time was ticking away,

'Only twenty minutes down this road' he said,

Dawn rolled her eyes, what type of response did he want from that information? The plan itself was simple but it did rely heavily on a story her mother told her as a child, unproven folklore if she was being true to herself. Her mother was devoted to her Vine, she was a constant, a Glimmer that based her whole life on her Vine, Dawn was not a constant, as was obvious from her current predicament, faith in her Glimmer varied, it was probably her scepticism, which she assumed she inherited from her absent father. This was another sticking point for Dawn, a psychologist would say that her absence of a father figure was a catalyst for her choice in men. Alas, to make this plan work she would need to become faithful, she would need to become a constant, it would be the only way to survive.

        *   *   *   *

The twenty minutes flew by. They had arrived. The mist hit Dawns face as she exited the car, the droplets fused to her skin creating a thin sheath of protection, it was hopeful but not practical. The walk to the top would take over an hour and Angelo would have to get back to get Raegan, so they needed to say their goodbyes. Although Dawn was sure this would not be an actual goodbye it still felt very real. Angelo circled the hood of the car to meet her at the passenger door, they were nineteen years old again, they were young, happy, they were planning their tying ceremony. That time felt an age ago, so much had happened in the last six years, unimaginable things. He stood only inches from her, this was the closest they had been in months, she didn't know what to say, there were hundreds of possible things, especially if this plan didn't work but nothing left her lips, she could barely meet her eyes with his, she could hear his breathing shallow as he conjured up his last words,

'Look, I know this wasn't quite what we had planned', Dawns eyes finally met his as they rolled acknowledging his attempt at humour.

'You could say that',

'But in some ways, I wouldn't change a thing', his finger clasped hers reassuringly. Dawn breathed in his words; she could feel herself crumbling inside.

'I know'.

'Now' Angelo said, 'Do you remember what we said?' she could, it was etched into her mind like a map, 'Remember there must be witnesses, without them this is all worthless'.

Dawn nodded silently taking one steady step backwards,

'Do you remember the other important point?' her mind went hazy for a second and then clarity,

'I remember' she replied.

'Time to go then', she continued, switching her serious demeanour for a jovial one. She turned away from the car to start the trip to the summit of the waterfall, her shoes already caked in soft soil as she moved further from the vehicle, she didn't want to turn around, but it was impossible not to. Eight years of history into nothing. The glance was fleeting, only nanoseconds but it said everything it needed to say. Within a few seconds the car sped off, the pain and urgency distinct in its engine, she was on her own.

CHAPTER 40

RAEGAN

Raegan's senses were acute, being so far into Leon territory made her Glimmer fragile. Devin had positioned his empire on the south side of town, his house stood elevated from the rest in a truly noble way; this was his terrain. His house was neither grand or thrifty, she expected lavish gold and luxurious leather but was greeted by discounted practical furniture, his tastes were simple, much like hers.

'Do I need to keep those on you? he said from the other room, 'I would like this to be a mutual relationship, but that depends on you'.

Raegan twisted her wrists, the clear plastic strips burrowed in deep, restricting the blood flow to her thumbs, her hands distorted as she struggled to force them through the small opening.

'I can hear what you are trying to do, and that is not going to help strengthen our relationship' he snapped, a shower of clatters from the kitchenette dampening his voice.

A kink formed in her stomach, her feet bonded to the floor as she fixated her concentration on her wrists, she had broken a large pane of glass with her Glimmer surely she could do something about two plastic ties. It started small and it wasn't easy to create, she struggled to draw together the energy she needed, the place was solitary, deserted, that was probably part of his plan, he didn't trust her, he didn't want to underestimate her abilities. Devin re-entered the room holding two tin cups, both steaming from the top, the gesture, whilst kind, only made Raegan feel more loyalty to her Vine, the smell made her homesick and regretful of her decision to come here. What was she thinking? Dom was free, she had succeeded in the plan, but something was keeping her here, if she really wanted to leave she could find a way. Devin placed the hot cup just short of her reach.

'Now, this isn't going to work if you don't have the use of your hands, I am going to cut one free, can I trust you not to do anything stupid?'

Raegan nodded her head, keeping her eyes low. Devin sat adjacent to her on a kitchen stool to maintain his height dominance, they sat together in total silence for over a minute, Raegan was settling in, testing the air between them, she looked up and caught his eye. She hadn't looked at him this closely, his eyes studied hers in the mutual seize fire. His brow sat heavy on his green eyes, not green like hers, they were misty green, their smoky appearance clouding her judgement, his hair was slightly thinning on the top but it was kept short, only millimetres from his scalp. To her he was a stranger but as her eyes explored his he felt more to her, she should be enraged with him, she should hate everything about him, but she didn't, she was strangely serene and at peace around him.

'So, what do you want to know kid? He asked

The quiet was broken and followed by a gaudy slurp, Raegan didn't respond, she didn't know what to ask, there were so many questions, too many questions. She politely raised the coffee to her lips and slurped. The sweet, milky fluid tingled in her mouth; she couldn't remember the last proper meal she ate.

'She was my everything you know', he said relaxing back against the wall,

'It was never going to be perfect, we knew that, but we were young and in love and nothing mattered but us' breathing deep he let the painful memories be revived in his mind.

'We had to keep our relationship a secret, it would never have been allowed, not by the Vine or the Bane, it was quite easy to begin with, we met up at pre-set times, sneaked out until dusk, the biggest issue of ours was evading her pathetic and cowardly consort, boy he kept his eyes open, he was suspicious and always a little jealous' he smirked with the last comment, Raegan scowled to indicate her distaste.

'Hey, you're young, you know what it's like, you don't want people, especially your elders telling you what to do, you feel invincible, we felt invincible'.

The ache intensified in his face, Raegan sensed a turn in the narrative, a flicker started to brew within her, pain began to seep from his being.

'I didn't even know what happened, she just stopped turning up, she avoided all of our usual spots and never went back to the diner, I was convinced she had been found out, someone knew our secret and was keeping her from me'

His tone changed from sad to manic,

'But that wasn't the case' his fists balled up against his torso.

'She had chosen not to see me, she was cutting me out of her life and I had no understanding of why, that's the really important part you have to understand Raegan, I was totally in the dark about everything',

Devin's heartbeat quickened, the flicker was starting to take shape, this could be her opportunity to escape, if she could establish the full flicker she may be able to convince him to let her go, she had to be subtle, careful and just let it happen naturally.

'I blamed myself for getting in too deep, I blamed my Bane for ruining my choices and keeping me in so tight, I blamed everyone except her' he continued throwing his head into his hands and sealing his eyes from view, embarrassed by his lapse in machismo.

'I spent weeks waiting for her, I turned up at the diner everyday hoping to see her, it wasn't like today, you couldn't just send a subtle text or follow her on social media, all of our communication was real, face to face, I didn't even phone her at her home, it was too dangerous, she had blocked my number at work so she never took the call. Then one day she did, I got fed up with her disregard, her ill-mannered ignorance towards me so I cold called her, she barely spoke but I did, I told her what would happen if she didn't speak to me, I warned her of the consequences but she didn't listen. After that, no words crossed our lips, the last time I called, I contacted her at home, Kane found the number for me but he answered the phone, he told me I wasn't good for her and I needed to leave them alone... them...' he repeated, disgust dripping from the final word.

'Them...I was furious, when did they become a 'them'. I lost control for a while after that, it was a dark time for me and I did some things I regret, things I can't take back, things that have shaped the man I have become, the man my people have grown to fear'.

Raegan had become so enraptured in the flicker she was missing the key parts of the story,

'Wait' she interrupted, 'You didn't know about me?',

'Not at first, it was only by chance I found out the truth, it had been so well hidden, she was being protected by the full Vine, making her invisible to me and everyone outside of it. Then it happened, I saw her, her belly swollen, engorged, my eyeballs locked at what I was seeing, Kane and Hayes saw it too, they grabbed my arms to stop me from confronting her, as I said I wasn't in a good place and they knew I couldn't be trusted to make the right choices'

His pain struck Raegan like a ball of nails and glass contorting inside his chest, she winced as he transferred the pain, the torture he had been carrying all of these years onto her like a speeding train, her mind was ambushed by a mirage of images, she saw the lady in the pictures at her Grans, her mother was happy, safe and affectionate, he let her feel the love they shared, it was comforting for a moment, until it fragmented into bitter pieces all swirling erratically around them. To the naked eye the room was still but between the two of them a storm was brewing.

'I thought I would control myself, I wanted to control myself, but my Leon instinct was too strong and I saw red, I instructed the Bane to march'.

Devin slumped onto the floor, his neck taut as he stared at the blankly at the ceiling, Raegan maneuvered her hand from the second tie, she was free but remained still in the chair, seizing the pain, she should have fixed it, taken it or numbed it, but something was blocking her, something dark filled her soul, her spirit heavy, her lungs drained.

'I didn't want her to leave Raegan' Devin insisted as he made his way to his feet,

'I wanted her to stay, I wanted us to work, I would have sacrificed my Bane for her',

The inner storm was now physically visible, the room spun, Raegan dropped to her knees, the flicker slowly withdrawing from her body, her legs solid as they moulded to the cold tiles, what was happening to her?

'We all knew the legend Raegan and that is why it was so important to keep you safe, and I will admit, she did a good job of that, but now it is time for you to find your Leon self and join your Bane'

Raegan's body coiled to the foetal position, her eyelids twitched forcefully as sharp pains travelled up her spine jolting through her skeleton and filling her bones with oblivion.

'The pain will end Raegan, but you have to let it in, you have to really feel it and then it will stop',

'What have you done to me?' she screeched, the pain forcing her into blackout,

Devin looked fondly at his Raegan, 'I'm bringing you home'.

CHAPTER 41

DAWN

It was so beautiful at the top, a gem in natures tapestry, Dawn stood against the wooden gate, her toes creeping towards the edge of the damp soil. A few wandering tourists roamed to the edge of the falls, cameras in hand, jostling for the finest picture, Dawn sensed each person there, her flickers materialising every few seconds. A woman called May was at the falls that day, she was seventy-two years old and she climbed the eight-mile hike to see her daughter every week. Her daughter's ashes were spread on a small bush with yellow and white blossoms, it was part of her healing ritual, she made the trek to separate her grief from her everyday life, she could come to this place and feel her pain then put it way until the next week. Dawn wanted to react to the flicker, she could see the memories, the happy times on vacation, her joy at the birth of her granddaughter, the agony of seeing her vibrant daughter waste away in front of her eyes, Dawn could take it all away, ease the pain for a short time but she didn't, she had to focus on what she came to do. She had chosen this spot very carefully and it was imperative that she kept to time, there was only going to be a three-minute window for this to work. The sun rose to its highest point reflecting its rays on the soft mist that clung kindly to Dawns clothes, alongside the brightness came the shadows and that was where she needed to focus her attention. She needed to take from the light and give to the dark, they were the last words that her mother had spoken when they designed the plan and she had carved them into her head. Taking another small step towards the edge she looked around for her witnesses, if she had been gifted with a stronger Glimmer she could have placed the memories in their minds without even moving but it wasn't the case, she would need to jump, they would need to see her do it for him to believe, he would check them carefully to ensure their memories weren't adjusted or manipulated, that's why they needed to be real. Dawn could not interfere with their flickers, it would show up, like a thumbprint or luminal liquid at a crime scene. Time continued to tick by, Dawn took a deep breath and gazed directly into the sun,

'This is for your Raegan, I hope to see you again soon',

The sound of the water muted, and the world stopped. Four sets of eyes froze, mouths gasped as they witnessed the young women jump into the centre of the falls, the water enveloped her pulling her into the shadows below. Two of the group started to make their way down the falls in an attempt to search for the woman, another used the lens of the camera as a set of binoculars, the last lady, May, just sat in shock with her head between her hands rocking back and forth until the rescue team arrived. They would never find a body, or even any evidence she was there, the only evidence was in the witness's memories. She was gone.

*   *   *   *

The emergency services took over thirty minutes to arrive, May stood at the foot of the falls, she hadn't taken her eyes away from the water since the incident, she stayed hopeful, looking deeply into the dark water for any signs of life, any murmurs of existence. The water hadn't rippled or wrinkled beyond the flow from the falls, she composed herself, her light breath mimicking the lack of oxygen the woman would be getting. Three illuminous bodies hurtled into the ice cold water in anticipation of the lifeless corpse, two fully suited divers followed, reversing into the current, splashing their long rubber feet, droplets speckled her eyeglasses enough for May to remove them to clean them. Her vision was blurred momentarily but long enough to catch a glimpse of the strange blazing light that lurked to the rear of the falls. She blinked her eyes to clear them and placed her eyeglasses back in their natural place, the light was gone. She pulled the frames from the top of her nose to blur her vision for a second time, eyes squinted towards the empty space, there was nothing, just the repeating spray of water hitting the surface. The other witnesses all spoke to the officer in charge describing what they had seen and how it had happened, May was approached to describe the woman as she has the best view of the incident. Her basic recall was quite accurate and would allow the police to create an image for the press, medium brown hair, slim build, wearing a black jacket and cropped jeans, she would leave out the small details but that would be enough for Angelo to come forward and claim her and for her Vine to grieve. It was cruel but necessary. Nobody would be found but the portrait of grief that her Vine would paint should be enough to convince Devin that it was true. After the debrief, May stayed at the scene, she felt she needed to guard it, she was not sure of what she was guarding against, but she was drawn to stay; enchanted to.

The day soon turned into dusk and a chill established in the air, May continued to watch over the deserted waterfall, police tape fluttered in the wind breaking the eerie silence. By the time night had fallen three sets of headlamps were driving erratically towards the location, their speed epitomised by the vulgar hum of their engines. The sound was unnerving, a feeling of dread pitted in Mays stomach as she concealed herself in the dense shrubbery. The cars pulled up to the bottom of the falls, six men exited the vehicles, dressed head to toe in black, a sense of urgency and impatience in their movements, torch lights sprayed sparks of light across the hillside as they clambered to the top. The first man to get to the top stood prominently as the others caught up, he was tall and well assembled in comparison to the rest. May remained quiet, not wanting to bring her presence to the attention of the men.

'Check everywhere' shouted the man,

'I need to be sure'.

The men scoured the water creating surges that pounded the shore, May didn't need to ask what they were looking for, she knew she needed to stay and this was why, something inside her had compelled her to.

'Hayes, trek to the top of the fall, make sure it's clear', the man responded with a disconcerted huff,

'Just do it!' he said gesturing his hands abruptly.

He stayed still, timid in his own space whilst the other men explored a mile around the falls, he wasn't using his body to search, he was hunting with his mind. Eyes closed, head tilted to the sky, May felt cold, detached and scared, it captivated her body, she pulled her limbs in tighter causing a break in the undergrowth, the man's eyes promptly glared her way, he couldn't see her but it was enough to disturb whatever he was focusing on, he stepped forward curiously aiming his gaze in her direction.

'Nothing' hollered the voice from the top of the falls distracting he man,

'Okay, Let's go' he shouted recalling all of the men, he was the last to make his way down the hill, gazing intensely into the falls before he made his final decline, May was sure she heard him whisper something but she couldn't make it out, she wasn't even sure it was in English, but whatever he said, it had broken his heart.

CHAPTER 42

DOM

Dom was blindfolded and dragged out of the room, his world went black, the material covered his nose making it his mouth uncomfortably dry. A whirlpool of anxiety swirled in his stomach as the two men shoved him into a car, the mixture of diesel and brake fluid gathered on this tongue as he fought to breathe through his mouth. As he lay awkwardly on the rear seat the events of the previous thirty minutes repeated in his head, Raegan was in trouble, he needed to warn someone, he was going to have to escape and get a message to Alice. Dom was wedged tight into the car; pressure was building in his legs as the two men slid into the front seats, ear-splitting beats boomed as the car engine rumbled, a loud shudder followed as the driver shoved the stick forward. Dom wriggled his body to pull the cloth from around his eyes, it settled on the top of his nose, the frayed edges distorting his vision, the windows were blacked out with only minimal light reaching him from the front. With a mumbled tone the men exchanged pointless conversations sandwiched with snippets of information about the upcoming journey, their muffled voices deafened by the loud music made it difficult for Dom to establish where he was or where he was going. As the car built up speed, he started to count the flashes of light to try to navigate his position in the town, he knew that as soon as the lights became further apart and eventually disappeared he would be in serious trouble. Devin wouldn't take a chance with him, he was too unpredictable and Raegan had swallowed his lie whole, not even questioning his agenda, fury grew in Dom's mind as he reflected on that point, How could she? How could she not care? How could she be so stupid as to believe he was going to let him go? A dark cloud festered over Dom as his Leon reflex kicked in, the veil of blackness permeated his skin, sewing the darkness in.

The music was so loud that the two men in the front of the car did not hear the commotion, Dom focused his mind on that one thought, the anger that had got him to this point. The ties on his hands began to liquefy from the heat his body was emitting, Dom could feel the plastic soften as he forced his wrists to separate. He stayed low in the car only making noise in time with the natural movements of the car, keeping his hands facing his back he stretched down to access the ties on his shoes, these would not be as easy to remove. Dom carefully slid off his left shoe, exposing his bare foot, he would need to wriggle his foot out of the restraints if he was going to make a run for it. The man in the passenger seat began glaring at Dom in the side mirror, he continued to thrash about convincingly trying hard not to reveal his advantaged position. Looking up he noted that the street lights were getting sparse and the road uneven, if he was going to escape he would need to do it soon or he would be too far away from town to warn Alice in time. His exposed foot cupped the door handle, using his big toe to release the door latch so he could edge out on the next bend, time slowed as he delayed his exit, for a second he contemplated not jumping, he could just let himself go, either in death or if he was lucky to escape at the final stop, he was filled with pain, terrible pain that seized his days and conquered his nights, a pain he thought he was to endure forever, until he met her. She lightened the agony, the sting that spread over him, reminding him of who he was and what he had done was numbed when she appeared in his life, even at the early stages of her Glimmer, it soothed him. The car turned viciously into the bend throwing Dom's weight away from the semi unlocked door, his head compressed against the faux leather door panel, his momentum allowing his body to propel out as the car began to increase its speed.

The impact would have been enough to kill him if it wasn't for the dense grasslands that rested alongside the highways, but the cushioning caused multiple burns to his torso. The roll out ended with Dom lying face down in the dry dirt, his head still spinning from the triple roll. Wrestling with his balance he scrambled to his feet, swaying and staggering from his hands and knees, the world was smeared, his eyes tried to focus and gain a sense of orientation. The car screeched to a halt, dust and gravel spitting from the wheels, Dom had only gained a few seconds in the pursuit, the two men shot out of the car and moved quickly to where Dom had landed, they were composing a visual symphony of the landscape, moving strategically through the undergrowth. Dom kept his breathing shallow, the burns on his body smouldering with his every step, the town lights sparkled in the distance, calling him home to safety, he could hear their heavy footsteps catching him, they wouldn't give up, they were trained not to. Dom had to make it to Glimmer territory, they wouldn't be welcome there and by now the Vine would have collected, it would be too dangerous for them. Dom's legs grew tired in the pursuit, his trousers ripped from the ankle exposing his bleeding skin. The Leon men continued to hunt him; perseverance ingrained in their biology. The vibrant city lights continued to show Dom the way but time was against him, who knew what Devin was doing to Raegan, he thought the worst and this thrust him forward, faster and stronger, his own survival instinct jolting him into reboot.

A set of unfamiliar footsteps entered the chase, they were light and nimble in comparison to the Leon steps but erratic in nature. Two sharp thuds echoed a few feet from Dom, he jerked to a halt directing his attention behind him, his heart paused in panic at the new addition in the hunt. It all went silent, not a whisper carried in the air, Dom's breathing returned as he hurled back into his stride, no one followed him now, he was alone. He reached the edge of the city, sweat and dirt violating the fresh air, he was confused about what had just occurred but indebted to whatever it was that saved him.

He didn't remember the rest of the journey, it was a hazy, obscured in the darkness, he reached a doorstep, his lungs begging for air as his legs perished beneath him. Heavy hands beat the door longing for someone to hear his plea, the door opened slowly, and Dom fell straight in, through peeping eyes he saw a tall, slender man approach him. Consciousness was not his friend forcing him in and out repeatedly over the subsequent minutes, Dom held on to small pieces of information trying to maintain his focus, but his mission was futile as unconsciousness cloaked him.

*   *   *   *

He was unsure how many hours had past but the sun was now breaking through the horizon. His whole body was sore, crippled in grass burns and bruises but soothed by linen bandages which smelt like lotion. His senses roused in the commotion in the adjoining room, a union of muffled voices bled through the plaster board walls, the pitch and frequency of the speech inferring a sense of panic, multiple accents and expressions uniting for a common cause. The place was familiar, but Dom had not been here before, the bed squeaked as he eased his weight vertically, his eyes gazing at the assortment of happy pictures staring back at him. This wasn't his experience of childhood, there were no happy pictures on his wall. The eyes of the young woman in the picture followed Dom as he moved towards the door, a kind face and caring appearance drew him in, he felt like he had met this woman before but could not place her. The door swung open taking Dom's breath away, a man stepped in, his presence potent, Dom didn't need to ask who he was, it was clear from his concerned expression he was on his side.

'We need to talk to you' he said, defeat coating his every word.

Dom nodded and followed him to the adjoining room, he was greeted by herd of eyes looking through him, a least fifteen people crowded into the small space, Dom felt lonely, his depravity obvious in the sea of light. Only one face stood out, Alice. She waved awkwardly, as if they were strangers, her eyes darting unnervingly from Dom to the young man standing a few feet from her. Before he could piece it together, a woman took centre stage gesturing her arms towards him,

'Won't you sit?' she said

'No, I'm fine thank you'

'Okay well, we will get straight to it, we believe you have come here to give us a message',

'I have, well sort of' he replied.

'What do you mean sort of?' blasted a voice from the side,

'Let him speak' commanded the lady in the centre.

'I only know part of the story. Raegan came to find me, Devin has been holding me for the last couple of days, I think he was holding me as bait',

'As bait? 'questioned the man still standing by the door. 'Why would he use you as bait?',

'Me and Rae are sort of friends,' Dom replied,

'Friends!' interrupted another voice,

'How can she be friends with you, Leon', animosity clouded the air as the whispering began, the woman in charge hushed the chatter.

'Did she find you? Did he hurt her?' she said more seriously this time.

'Yes she found me, he didn't hurt her from what I saw, I was taken away for dead only moments after she arrived', the crowd gasped in anticipation of his next sentence,

'She gave herself to replace you, he took her in your place?' said the younger man through his teeth.

'He didn't take her, she stayed, I told her to leave, I begged her to go but she didn't listen, he told her he was going to release me but I knew that was never going to be the case, so I escaped from their car and ran straight here'.

'How did you know where we were?' questioned the woman,

'I don't know, I was compelled, I followed the light, but then I passed out'.

Silence smothered the chatter, their internal connections uniting to carefully keep Dom in the dark about the discussion, only the odd glare from person to person was shared in the subsequent minutes, Alice stood as baffled as Dom was, their alien selves uncomfortable amongst the Vine.

'He knows' chanted a voice from the back of the room,

'It is done' she continued, the atmosphere in the room turned wretched, spoilt by those three simple words. Disbelief settled over the once hopeful Vine; Alice moved to the centre of the room.

'We don't know for sure' she said,

'I've seen it' the woman stated back,

'Seen what?' questioned Dom,

The group turned their backs in disgust, ignoring his plea for information, all except two. Alice and James both stayed focused on Dom, they knew he wasn't the enemy and that he was also the best chance of finding Raegan alive. Alice reached inside her back pocket pulling out a tattered piece of discoloured paper, its lifespan obviously near to an end. She handed it to Dom. The crumpled folding had worn parts of the diagram, but the message was clear as day, Dom was now in on the secret, when his eyes returned to the room the Vine joined him in his sorrow,

'We can't let her go' Dom shouted, his grief resonating in his words, 'We have to get her back' he continued,

'We all want that too, but we are going to need you to help us'.

CHAPTER 43

RAEGAN

When the pain numbed Raegan slept, a deep and dreamless sleep that lasted for hours, her body recovering from the trauma of change, she awoke in a room she did not recognise, the air was different, dry and sticky all at once. She rolled from her side to sitting, head spinning as she adjusted to the new environment. No one else was present but Raegan wasn't scared, she opened the wooden door shifting her weight forward to see who else was the house. Part of her knew who was with her, she could sense him, she could sense him the same way she could sense her Vine, except they were gone, that's how she knew that they were not near her town, the connection had been severed. The place was small, dishevelled, it hadn't been lived in for years, white linen sheets covered the small amount of furniture that was there. Spirits of memories scattered the room in the shape of dust shadows, things had been moved recently that was clear. Raegan walked towards the open window, the place was peaceful, the sun shone on every inch of the land lighting up each blade of dry grass, she took in a long breath, inhaling the natural world, capturing a long overdue moment peace.

'This is where you were born Raegan' said Devin from the corner of the kitchenette, she turned, startled by the disturbance,

'You were born into his arms only meters from where we both stand; I imagine it was a very joyful occasion for them. I wasn't invited as you well know' his sarcasm attempting to cover up the pain.

'She was only doing what she thought was best' Raegan replied,

Devin creased up in over exaggerated laughter, his mocking tone saturating the room.

'You still defend her Raegan, even now. She left you, abandoned you to a man who has no biological link to you because she was weak and scared',

'She was scared of you' Raegan shouted back, a small tear gathering in the corner of her eye. 'She feared the father of her child, what does that say about you?'

Her fingertips began to tingle, sending pulses through her veins, a crescendo of pain assembling in her core.

'Whoa' said Devin looking at Raegan like she was a new toy. She composed herself, aware of what he was trying to achieve.

'Why did you bring me here?' she commanded turning the focus back to the current situation,

'I wanted you to see this' he said relaxing back into a wicker chair.

He pointed pompously towards the wall at the rear of the kitchen, a smirk of knowing settling on his face, Raegan turned to see a small note pinned loosely to the wall, her focus adjusted as she moved slowly towards it. A delicate scribbling of ink rested on the paper, Raegan tilted her head to decipher the slanted text,

'I can't do this… look after my Rae of sunshine, Dawn x'.

Raegan was puzzled.

'She left you once before' said Devin, sneering like the cat who got the cream, the words ricocheted like bullet fragments in Raegan's mind,

'When?' shot out of her mouth before she had time to process her own thoughts,

'When you were three months old, or ninety-two days to be exact'.

A torrent of uncertainties submerged Raegan's emotions, stunned, her reflexes momentarily anesthetised by his declaration. An obscure darkness encircled her, invoking an inner presence ripping her soul in two. Devin stood up and put his hands in his back pockets, his posture coaxing the darkness that was embodying Raegan.

'This is you Raegan, I saw it in you years ago, you won't remember me but I was always there, at a distance', the sentiment was supposed to indulge her but all it did was trigger more questions,

'Then you are just as bad as her, she was trying to leave me and you didn't even show up',

Fury raged in her voice, spitting the words viciously towards him. The floorboards began to shake, the loose nails shivering in their beds creating friction sparks, dark thoughts buried themselves deep in Raegan's soul, tunnelling like cyclones in storm, she didn't push them out, she let them burrow, she let the pain in. She was an unwanted child, uninvited in conception, unwelcome at birth and repeatedly abandoned by those who were supposed to take care of her.

'That man who has no biological link that you speak of is the only person in my world that has been constant, so don't belittle him to me' she yelled

Windows shattered with her final syllable, splinters of glass lingered in the air momentarily as the walls around the two of them collapsed, plasterboard crumbling like icing on a wedding cake. The sun was now hidden by an array of angry clouds, Raegan and Devin were stranded in the carcass that was once a house. Raegan glanced to the sky, cyclones formed aiming their eyes in Devin's direction, a gust of wind followed with dense rain for dessert. Devin stood in awe of Raegan; he hadn't imagined this.

'I'm not the enemy Raegan, they kept you from me, they knew your potential but chose not to tell you' he hollered though the thick storm, rain beating brutally against his face.

'I am the only one who was willing to tell you the truth and give you a chance to make your own choice' he hollered with a level of genuineness in his tone. Raegan tried to use her Glimmer to map him, but it was impossible, that part of her was deactivated.

'You can't use that on me Raegan, she couldn't so you never will' he continued.

The cyclones crept closer bringing devastation with them until Raegan conceded, broken by the complexities of her existence. The weather returned to its exquisite wonder leaving the two strangers solitary in the ruins.

'I don't want you to leave' said Devin.

The first sense of sincere emotion edging subtly into his voice since they met.

'On one condition', replied Raegan pulling her wet hair away from her face,

'You tell me where she is'.

Moving through the debris left from the storm Devin lowered his head to the ground in defeat,

'She's dead Raegan'

Raegan looked directly into the whites of his eyes, he truly believed it, but she knew different.

CHAPTER 44

JAMES

The commotion had settled and quiet commenced, the three older women had left the room and were congregating in the kitchen, indistinct words though muffled voices drifted into the living area, James had remained still since Dom had entered the room, he was all in for rescuing him, until he met him. Something made him feel nervous, he didn't entirely trust him or his story, something about his version of events didn't quite add up. Why would Raegan choose to stay there if Dom was being released? The whole plan was based around getting him out. James' mind swirled with possibilities, was Dom lying? Or did Raegan have another agenda that she hadn't shared? Both alternatives were equally as likely, Raegan was not the best at sharing and James had not spent enough time with her to read her very well.

The meeting in the kitchen dragged, more and more people were arriving at the flat, Dom was sat in the corner of the room accompanied by Alice, their whispers inaudible to James. His periodic gazes towards the duo created bubbles of anxiety in his stomach, what were they sharing? Were they talking about him? The proximity between them decreased as the conversation became more intense, James could sense this from the pitch of Alice's voice, he didn't want to interfere but a flicker was building up inside him and as much as James wanted to control it he was not sure that could. His hands began to tingle sending shivers through his arms, flashes of light and vivid sketches saturated him, James tried to resist them, he didn't want to intrude on Alice's mind, especially as he was uneasy about what he might find. The pressure became intense as the flicker forced itself upon him, his resistance triggered pain. Glimmers were supposed take on flickers not to abstain from them, bolts of spasm hit him hard, each strike more painful than the last. James had never resisted for this long and the agony was slowly breaking down his defences, as his last guard of armour fell the room was filled with traffic, the three women had re-entered the room breaking the flicker and releasing James from his torture. The oldest women took the centre of the room commanding attention in her stance, the hush interrupting the intensity between Alice and Dom.

'We need to call the Vine' she announced,

'We need to shape a cluster Glimmer to save Raegan, it is the only way',

Mutters of disbelief filled the room.

'Can we do that?' questioned a young woman from the rear of the room, her hair long and curly at the ends, thick glasses obscuring her pretty face. 'Surely the risks of shaping a cluster Glimmer are too great? And we cannot guarantee it will work.'

The mutters turned to chatter and the chatter to yelling as each Glimmer tried to have their say. James threw his hand over his ears, he knew what a cluster Glimmer was, he had studied it in his first year as a Glimmer, and he had learned about it the hard way. Above the uproar came an intrigued voice,

'What's a cluster Glimmer?'

Dom's words deadened the room, twenty sets of eyes all glaring in the same direction, he stood up, his head raised above most of the people in the room. The women in the centre fumbled for the shoulder of the older man who stood in front of her, he guided her to Dom, she rested her hand on his.

'A cluster Glimmer is when we all work together to create a flicker to map a Leon. None of us here are natural Mappers so none of us can do it alone, but when we work together as a Vine, we can create one' she said calmly,

'But it's not that simple' hollered the lady from the back. 'It is very risky for all of us, we will make ourselves vulnerable, incapable of defending ourselves should it go wrong, plus we are not just talking about your average Leon, we are talking about Devin',

'We have no other choice', the lady replied keeping her hand in Dom's.

'He will help us'.

CHAPTER 45

RAEGAN

He hadn't spoken to her since they left the wilderness, the journey back had been in silence, his eyes focussed on the road ahead as if Raegan wasn't there. They took a different route on the way back, heading east on 47 instead of northeast, Raegan didn't question it, she didn't dare speak, his temper lethal and delicate at the same time. After thirty minutes of detour from the main highway Devin finally pulled into the next town, it was unfamiliar to Raegan. They drove carefully into the main street, Raegan surveyed the people walking through their normal day, just doing normal things, a pang of jealously struck hard, she had lost track of her version of normal, her life had changed so much in such a short space of time that her normal was unrecognisable. Devin indicated left and turned the car into a separate side passage, the mottled grey brickwork fused with old school graffiti; hate and love declared passionately in the jumbled words. Time had worn the text and symbols, but the passion was still alive, it bled from the walls as the car jerked impatiently to a standstill. Devin continued the silent treatment outside the car, only signalling his demands through small eye gestures. Raegan pushed the heavy door extending her legs from the car, the air felt thick in her lungs as she took her place in the alley, Devin was a few meters in front moving purposefully down the passageway.

Raegan hurried her steps to catch up, intrigued by the enigmatic journey she was taking, the alleyway began to swallow them as the darkness enclosed around them, a knot of thorny butterflies swarmed in her stomach as her adrenaline kicked in. The further they walked the more sets of eyes appeared in the windows, there was no red carpet but she felt like this had all been planned, she had played into his hands, he had predicted her every move. Raegan was conflicted, on one hand she was angry at herself for falling into this world but on the other hand flattered by the attention. The doors at the end of the passage opened on command, a light chorus of voices echoed in the closed space, Raegan could not decipher the words but the whispers carried a warmth, but it felt immoral, impure, soiled by an appetite for more. The eyes that watched her changed, she no longer felt flattered, gluttony invaded them with Raegan feeding their insatiable emptiness.

'This way' said the young scrawny man standing guard at the doors,

'Where are we?' she questioned; he did not reply.

The walls inside the building were stripped back, rudimentary in comparison to the outside, her footsteps echoed against the cold floor tiles building in tempo as she moved through the building. The crowd parted in unison, a movement they rehearsed and performed with untimely grace, Raegan was drawn into their dance, watching with precision as they glided into their set formation. Devin moved into the centre of the crowd, he was their quarterback in a complicated game,

He spoke like a ringmaster. 'Thank you for your courtesy, today I bring a guest with me, a very special guest, someone you have waited over a decade to meet'.

Raegan shuffled her feet, a figurative spotlight beaming down, her anxiety slowly bubbling in apprehension of her solo performance.

'This is Raegan' he announced proudly. Any eyes that hadn't been focused on her before were now fixated in her direction,

'She is my daughter'.

*　　　　*　　　　*　　　　*

The rest of the day was a haze, Raegan met so many new people she couldn't store all of their names in her head. Her Glimmer had been working overtime as she waded through a symphony of gossip and sentiment, each tale more vivid than the last. Devin had watched her for hours, he sat idle just meters from her. After everything she had been told about him she was starting to become fond of him, his protrusive confidence was contagious and Raegan was contaminated. It was strange how someone she had feared so viciously could now be easing into her life, she had been overwhelmed by the kindness of all of the people she had met, their raw compassion for life puzzled her, this was not the world she had been warned about, or the world that Dom had described so eloquently and with so much sorrow.

'They're all yours Raegan, each and every one of them' he said,

'What do you mean they are mine? how can they be mine? They are individual people, with lives, most which I have clearly seen today'.

He didn't reply quickly, instead he mulled over his words, selecting them carefully,

'Well, if you want to phrase it differently, you are theirs' his words muddied the water even further.

'You are part of them Raegan and they are part of you, you are kin. Leon kin are not just linked by blood, much like Glimmer, we are connected by something deeper, something ingrained deep in our DNA, and you are part of that bloodline Raegan. It is something that has been kept from you, something you have been told is wicked and evil but I am here to tell you that what you have been sold is a lie'.

His monologue cleared the room, except for one small girl sitting cross legged on the hard floor, her clothes were worn, scuffed shoes coated her small feet, her distracted mind focused on the object cupped in her hand, she was oblivious that the room had cleared, lost in her own little world. Devin summoned the young girl with a distinct whistle, she hurried towards them like a puppy to its master.

'Klaudia, this is Raegan' he said,

Raegan lowered herself to the meet the eye-line of the girl.

'Hi' she said awkwardly, Devin joined the duo placing his hand on her shoulder,

'Raegan is your little sister'

The words dropped like bombs, he was watching for a reaction, waiting to see what would happen, another test.

'Klaudia, that's a pretty name' she said keeping her breathing steady and in control knowing that any slight murmur of shock could trigger a Glimmer or worse.

The girl had beautiful eyes, deep and dreamy, two brewing hurricanes staring straight back at her, she didn't look like Raegan, her hair was darker and thinner and her face was rounder, whether this was the twinkle of youth or genetics was unclear.

'Nice to meet you' said Klaudia sweetly as she skipped out of the building,

'She is yours too' said Devin proudly.

Time had seeped away and as Raegan left the building she was greeted by a dusky sky. Looking into the dying sun she remembered what she was supposed to be doing, she absorbed the beams of warmth into her skin recalling the day's events.

'One last thing to show you' said Devin pointing towards a rusty iron door at the top of the steps.

Raegan was growing weary of his games, but her intellect was abducted by her curiosity, she followed him to the top of the stairs, each step creaking beneath their weight. The room was poorly lit, so it was difficult to see anything of value, Devin walked into the centre and turned to face Raegan.

'This has been really difficult for me Raegan, having you here, in this sacred place, I want to trust you, I want you to be part of this, to take your place in your true home' his voice sounded genuine.

'But although I trust half of your genes, I know not to trust the other half',

Before Raegan could respond a sharp pain pierced the side of her neck, warm fluid surged down her spine pooling in a warm fuzz in her hands and feet. She lost her sense of gravity and plummeted towards the floor; two pairs of hands cushioned her fall bringing her gently to the ground. She was barely conscious and she commanded all of her control to stay in the zone, she had been baited into a trap, tricked into a false sense of security, the voices gradually distorted as Raegan lost her battle with consciousness. Devin knelt beside her brushing the tangled orange hair from her cheek, for a split second she felt it, a flicker of something, her Glimmer ached for more, searching blindly inside him for some humanity, something to show he was more than just a Leon. Her search was fruitless but as she slipped into darkness, she thought about her, the other half of her gene pool that had hurt this man so terribly that he felt he needed to do this. She did this to him, she did this to them both.

CHAPTER 46

DAWN

13 years later

She stared at the checkout laser anesthetised by its red glare, one beep after the next, a conveyer belt of boredom edging towards her one item at a time. She often compared her own life to that conveyer belt, edging away her sanity one day at a time.

'Heather' shouted a young woman from behind the customer services desk, nobody replied.

'Heather' she shouted louder this time, Dawn sprang into action,

'Yes' she turned to the women, who was considerably younger than Dawn, a college graduate that walked into the superior role. Dawn could never do that, she had to keep under the radar, she had to be *Heather*. *Heather* was a checkout adviser; adviser was put onto the title to make it sound like a more prosperous career choice than it was. *Heather* didn't socialise with her work colleagues, she didn't really know anyone, not properly, she couldn't risk giving too much way and she didn't want to get close to anyone, her heart couldn't take it, it was bruised, scarred by the trauma from her youth. No person should have to go through what she had been through.

'Heather, we need you on aisle four' repeated the voice,

Disgruntled by this request Dawn closed her cash desk and drifted towards the aisle, her feet moving robotically, separate to her brain. Dawn had kept her Glimmer a secret from everyone around her, but it had consequences, her Glimmer was sedated, she had pushed so many flickers away that she barely felt them anymore. When Dawn first emerged from hiding her flickers were erratic, the long-term hibernation she had cocooned herself in had created a shield, impenetrable from flickers. It was not natural. Dawn was not even aware it was possible, but it was what she needed to do to survive and her new life was purely about survival.

Aisle four could only have a set number of variables; shelf stacking, spillage (hopefully not of the body fluid type) or actual assistance (which was very rare). Dawn gambled these variables every time she was called away from the checkout. When she arrived at the top of the aisle a woman was standing holding a can of dried beans, she was not one of the regular customers, in fact Dawn didn't recognise her, which in itself was strange. The woman was studying the tin can intensely, maybe hoping it held the key to the universe, realistically she was probably asking if it was vegan friendly which was the current question trend in the store.

'How can I assist you today?' Dawn quoted in her most interested voice,

'I'm sorry to bother you, my daughter is blending food for my Granddaughter and…' her sentence cut off dead, her eyes glazed over cloudy and mysterious, Dawn tapped the woman's arms contemplating radioing for medical assistance.

'Dawn you need to return…you need to return urgently…he has her'. The woman's voice was cold and monotone, these were not her words, she was the messenger, the words were coming from somewhere else, somewhere familiar, somewhere she swore she would never return to. The woman's eyes returned to their normal colour, her complexion slightly paler than before, she was unaware of what had just occurred.

'…are these beans suitable for a 6-month-old or is there too much sodium?' but when the woman looked up Dawn was gone, vanished from sight, as if she had never been there. The cluster had been sent from her mother, they had promised to have zero contact unless it was a life or death situation because of the risks to the Vine so Dawn knew this was serious. She had hardly taken a breath since she had fled the store, her apron slung onto the sidewalk, unloved and neglected, her feet moving faster than they had in years, she didn't have a plan, but she didn't want one, having a plan would make her vulnerable and predictable, surprise was one of the only assets she had at this point. Breathless and sweaty she entered her third-floor apartment, she needed to travel light, take just what she could carry, she rummaged through her primitive belongings only grabbing what was essential. Clothes sailed through the air, a concoction of pastel lingerie and odd socks scattered the floor as she shoved things into the satchel. Delving deep into the bottom draw, her hand fumbling the joints that held the wood together, her finger pressed hard against the back revealing a small sculptured square of wood, it was engraved but not in English, it was something she had not held in her palm for over a decade, this is how she would find Raegan, now she just needed to work out how to get home.

CHAPTER 47

DOM

Everyone in the apartment was fixed, concentric circles of Glimmers knelt on the hard floor, physically motionless but a melody of energy danced in the air, Dom was not accustomed to such positivity, he had grown up in a bleak place, surrounded by deprivation. His family had transferred to Shaylock when he was young, before all this had occurred, he was scouted by Devin within days of his arrival, hand-picked to be part of the superior Bane at only 6 years old, pushed out by his mother and drawn into Devin's hold. Dom and Alice were not the only two left out of the cluster, they sat awkwardly at the side of the room watching the spectacle unfold whilst Angelo stared out of the back window. Dom was unsure why he was not involved, he was her father, much closer to her than most of the people in the room. The cluster started to sway side to side, just very subtly at first but then more intensely, Angelo looked at his watch, impatience in his eyes, waiting for something or someone to arrive. The mood changed unexpectedly when a sudden jolt of power surged through the room shorting the circuits and plunging the street into blackness. Alice gasped nervously, fumbling around in her space to comfort her disorientation, Dom was not as uneasy, he felt calm and relaxed in the darkness. No one spoke in reaction to blackout, so Dom assumed this was expected, maybe it was what Angelo was waiting for.

'It's done' announced Raegan's Gran as she pushed herself to standing 'The Vine has been called and will be here within the hour'.

'Did you reach her?' said Angelo still waiting impatiently by the window,

The cluster dispersed from the room finding their own pockets of space to recharge leaving just the five of them.

'It's done' she repeated, this time with a curt tone, obviously not wanting to repeat herself again. Dom was confused by the malice in the statement.

'You said the same earlier... but we still have nothing' said Angelo

Dom could sense the pressure building between the pair, something unspoken was being exchanged and James was caught in the crossfire. Disorientation surrounded him; Dom could see the confusion envelop James as he tried to piece together the fragments of information that were striking him.

'What is going on?' Alice screamed breaking the struggle between the trio. 'Will someone please explain to me to what is going on!'

Dom clasped her hand tenderly to diffuse her frustration, James' eyes followed the clutch watching carefully as Alice echoed the gesture.

'You need to tell them' blurted James breaking his focus on the duo,

'Tell us what?' said Dom prompting a look of trepidation in Angelo.

James took the lead, closing the internal doors to minimise the risk of the information leaking beyond the room.

'She's still alive' said James.

Dom still did not understand.

'Who is still alive?'. Angelo directed his attention back to the window,

'Dawn is still alive, she's Raegan's mother'.

The only gasp came from Alice, this was not new information to three of the people in the room, Dom was stunned, so many lies had been told, so much deceit.

'Raegan needs to know' Alice yelled towards them. 'She thinks her mother is dead'

'She knows' replied James,

'She has known since Dom and her absconded a few days ago, the story you told her about Devin got her thinking, then when she escaped at school from the Leon kin she saw her, just in a flash but it was enough'.

'How do you know this James? said Raegan's Gran, 'Did she tell you?'

'No, I saw it too, before I even met Raegan I started seeing things, strange things that didn't make sense to me, but my flickers have always been irrational so I didn't question them, not until now'.

'The true sign of matched consorts' murmured Angelo, 'We had it too' his voice breaking at the words.

'Until she severed it'.

Severing a consort tie triggered the most agonising pain, similar to how soulmates describe the feeling of a broken heart. It was something that Angelo and Dawn hadn't discussed before she left, they just accepted that was how it was going to be. The pain had dulled over the years but had resurfaced in past three days, fresh like the day it happened. Dom had thought that Angelo was staring out of the window looking for someone when he was trying to control the intense pain that was rendering his body of little use.

'If she is alive then where is she?' said Alice,

'I don't know' Angelo replied, the tip of his words cut with discomfort. 'I don't know how far away she was; I think she was still in the country, but she could be hours away',

'And she may not even come' said Alice with a sour tone.

The truth descended on the group, they really had no clue if Dawn would respond or not, maybe she had settled into a new life with a new family, maybe it was not as easy as picking up and leaving. Dom moved towards the small picture frames filling the plain cream wall, Dawns eyes following him as he got closer, he looked deep into her eyes, he saw slithers of Raegan looking back at him.

'I think she is already here' said Dom, his memory sparked by the small details on the images. 'I think she was the one that got me here yesterday, the Leon's were in pursuit, catching up on me minute but minute and then they were gone, two loud thuds and there was no one behind me, I was lost and confused, I don't know how I even made it here, it was like my body just knew which direction to travel, like I had been taken over by another force'.

When he had finished his confession Angelo grasped his shoulders, tightening his grip around him to breath in his energy.

'It was her' he concluded, 'She is here'.

What should have been a joyous moment was shrouded by the realisation that she hadn't appeared to the Vine.

'Did you see where she went Dom?' said Alice,

'No idea, as I said I can't really remember anything, just fragments'

A knock on the door broke the tension in the room, the first wave of Glimmers from the cluster call had arrived, seven additional bodies squeezed into the small apartment, Raegan's Gran greeting them like old friends. Dom's attention was drawn back to Angelo now folded over in pain by the window.

'What can I do?' asked Dom,

'Find her, you need to find her, we need to be tied again or I will be no use to anyone',

'I   will   do   my   best'.

CHAPTER 48

RAEGAN

Her body was heavy when she woke, thoughts dusty and muffled by the commotion surrounding her. Devin paced the room, his long strides purposefully telling their own story, he was anxious, she could sense it. She touched her neck where the needle had injected, it was sore but not swollen, shifting her weight she struggled to sitting, dizziness clouding her perception. More and more people entered the room walking straight past, as if she wasn't even there. Mutters and whispers turned into shouts and screams as the people crammed into the airless room, Raegan became uncomfortable in her space. Booted feet trampled on her as she struggled to stand, her small frame being pushed and shoved by the hordes of people congregating around Devin.

'They have called it, they have started this, but we will finish it' Devin hollered into the crowd,

Each word punctuated for maximum impact followed by a melodic cheer in response. Raegan didn't recognise these people, these were not the people she had been introduced to yesterday, these people hid dark thoughts, violence and brutality carved willingly into their minds. These were not the sweet and fragile souls to which she had been acquainted with only hours earlier. Raegan pushed her way through, clambering past the sour mix of savagery that stood in her path, the Bane were preparing to march.

'What are you doing?' she bellowed, her voice carrying above the raucous crowd.

All the eyes in the room turned to look for the voice that challenged their noble leader. Devin strode towards her, self-confidence exuding from every orifice.

'You cannot put this on me Raegan, I did not start this, they have called the Vine to challenge us, we cannot just sit here and let that happen' his words cut deep, sewing seeds of fear in her and loyalty into them.

'You are going to fight with us' he continued,

'Fight with you? How can you expect me to do that, they are my family', she spat back, insolence coating her words.

Devin took a moment to pause, the crowd hushed awaiting his reaction, their boisterous energy muffled in apprehension.

'I am your family, I have shown you what they have done to us, how they have continually crushed us, humiliated us with their control. I have a chance now to put this right, we have a chance Raegan' he meant the words he was speaking, he truly believed that ending the Glimmer would restore the Leon reign. It was the first honest thing he had said since they had met.

'I can't let you do that' said Raegan, blood slowly bubbling in her veins triggering a distracting tingling sensation down her spine,

'Let me' he jeered, prompting a wild laugh from the congregation.

'I don't need your permission' he said

His change of tone encouraging the crowd to snigger, he was playing the showman to invalidate her to the Bane, a gloating sneer expanding across his face, this was the side of Devin her mother ran away from and that Dom had warned her about, a cock sure thug, not the mild gentleman he had marketed himself as in the previous days.

'Confine her' he said without a second thought.

Four hands appeared from nowhere grabbing at her limbs, grappling with her squirming torso, she became a dull sound in the background as she screamed for release. The Bane was preparing to march, she needed to stop them. Raegan had learnt that anger was not a safe emotion for a Glimmer but she was running out of options, she couldn't risk being put into confinement, her arms and legs thrashed as she was escorted out of the building. They clung on tightly leading her down the steep metal steps into the basement of the building, the walls were wet with damp trickling onto the stone floor, a single bulb hung lonely from the ceiling emitting a dim light. Raegan focused on it, its faint light illuminating the dark room. She stretched a flicker out to reach one of the Leon henchmen, but it ricocheted straight back, a shielded glaze protecting them from her efforts, he had thought of everything. She tried again, pushing her Glimmer more forcefully but to no avail, it was impossible to get to them directly.

To quieten her mind she stopped thrashing, her dead weight become more awkward for the two men to manoeuvre, the energy she conserved could be harnessed to her advantage, the bulb whose light was so weak could refract her Glimmer into the men if she could focus all of her energy into it. Her decent to the cellar was almost complete, she could still hear the congregation on the upper floor, they hadn't left yet so she had time, she waited clutching onto seconds in a bid to boost the potency. Reaching the bottom of the stairway the men flung Raegan to the floor, just an off cut in their wondrous plan. She hit the floor hard but didn't really feel it, she was past feeling physical pain, her internal pain was much stronger than any physical pain she could be subjected to. As the two men started to climb the stairs to re-join the Bane one paused on the third step.

'Come on Tye, Devin is waiting for us, he's ready to march'

Tye did not reply, he stood on the step immobilised, the other man reached for his shoulder to jolt him to his senses, Tye was not going to move, he was no longer in control of his body, Raegan raised herself to standing and without saying a word commanded Tye to grab the other man's shirt and pull him in close.

'What are you doing? Get off me' he yelled

Tye did not release his grip, not without Raegan's permission, his eyes were glazed and his actions robotic, he jerked backwards pulling both men into an instant tumble. Raegan carefully moved aside to let the men through, their muscles entwined into a heap on the floor, Raegan's mapping had worked, and she had kept control of it. She hurried to the top of the stairs and back into the crowded room. Swiftly grabbing a black hooded jacket from the floor to conceal herself she paced towards the exit, her movements quick enough to make progress but not so quick as to rouse attention. She was thinking about so many things that she did not notice the tiny girl appear in the doorway, her hair in two untidy plaits glued unhygienically close to her head, not many things could delay Raegan but those small curious eyes stopped her in her tracks.

'Where are you going?' said Klaudia her voice angelic and inviting,

'I've got to get out of here' Raegan replied moving her face close to the scruffy girl.

'Where will you go?' the sweet voice questioned,

'Home'.

'This is your home'. Her words wise beyond her years, she bent down to her level.

'I know you think that, but I can't stay here, it is not who I am'

Raegan became aware of the quiet that surrounded her, the noise dispelled leaving an acoustic void in its wake.

'You are remarkable Raegan' Devin's voice rich with pride.

'You are unstoppable, no man can stand in your path', Raegan turned, his compliments lost on her,

'You can't keep me here, I won't stay' she said

'True' he replied, his hands fidgeting in his pockets,

'I won't make you stay, but you will want to be here by the time this is all through, nothing you do Raegan will make me turn you away, I will not abandon you because of who you are and what you can do',

His reference clearly pointing towards her mother's untimely desertion. Raegan pondered on that point, as a Leon she was accepted for who is was, not judged by the mistakes she had made or forced into being someone she didn't want to be. It was an attractive offer, but she couldn't consider herself Leon when it was the reason that her Mother did what she did. It would be an act of treachery on her part. The little girl clasped Raegan's hand in a desperate attempt to stop her leaving, her intensions very different from Devin's but still as toxic.

'I'll be seeing you soon' he stated, fully confident of his conviction.

He turned his back and strode towards the Bane, Raegan walked away in the opposite direction and she didn't turn back, not even to see the two small eyes tracing her every movement. She shouldn't feel bad about leaving but something in her gut was amiss, it trespassed her mind weaving doubt within her. She wouldn't be returning here, but her confidence was split, now she had taken her place as Leon leaving was not easy. She needed to be strong and get back to her Vine, she needed to see her Dad, Alice, her Gran and Dom, she had so much to tell them, so much to share about her true-self, but what if they didn't accept her? What if they could sense her allegiance to Leon and then banish her from the Vine. The decision to leave did not feel as clear cut now, she turned onto a side path that ran alongside the main road, hands shaking, she couldn't be rejected again, not by her own Vine.

Her back poised against the brick wall she slid her body down to the ground, she had only been walking for five minutes but she was already re-examining her choice. How did he know this would happen? They barely knew each other yet she felt that he knew better than anyone. Composing herself and bringing her breathing back in check she started back on her journey, the reaction to her return was unpredictable but if she didn't go, she would never know. She would not make the same mistake her Mother did, she would not take away the chance for people to accept her for who she was. Making her way to feet she filled herself with cheerful thoughts, she needed to give her Glimmer a chance to recover, she needed to reclaim her place on her Vine. Walking back to the main road she held one image in her head, when this was all over, she would go back for Klaudia;   that   is   no   place   to   raise   a   child.

CHAPTER 49

DAWN

The town was visible in the distance, her slight detour to help the boy escape from the two Leon's was just a warm up for Dawn, she had twelve years of pent up aggression to let out and enacting it on Kane and Hayes was very satisfying. As she got closer to the edge of town she could smell home, a concoction of tin, sweet lilac and dust all mixing together to give the town its flavour, it was something she hadn't experienced in years and it left a bittersweet taste in her mouth. She hadn't considered, beyond the immediate danger, the consequences of her current choices and how it would impact the Vine, she didn't even know if she would be welcomed back. The hardest part would be seeing him after all these years, Leon are notoriously unforgiving and finding out Dawns death was staged would only fuel the resentment.

Standing at the crossroads that separated the two parts of the town she felt cowardice, she should have been stronger, she should have been braver, so many of her decisions seemed selfish now, she had changed so may lives all to only delay the inevitable. Her little Raegan deserved better, she deserved more than the spineless mother she had been given, she wondered what she looked like, how well the genes had split, was she kind? Was she confident? All things she wished she could have instilled in her daughter as she grew up. Angelo would have done a good job; he wouldn't have let her become a cruel person. How did she cope with her first Glimmer? Was she a steerer like Dawn or did the Leon in her reduce her to a watcher? How much Leon did she have? Had she even converted to Leon yet? The questions filled the time it took for her to reach her home street, it was eerily quiet, uncomfortably so, the usual bustle of the evening was not present tonight. The place had changed in the decade she was missing, but only partly. The houses were the same except some of them had now been converted into flats, the shops were still there but most were now coffee joints or fast food outlets. There was a light on in the window of her mother's apartment, the same light (and probably bulb) she had gazed at in her teens as she slithered through the front door to avoid detection. Nausea set in as she took the final few paces to the cobbled steps, they were the same safety hazard they had been all those years ago, the last few occurring in slow motion, this was not a place Dawn thought she would ever return to. Before she could reach her hand up to press the buzzer a familiar face greeted her from side path.

'We weren't sure that you would come' said Angelo exhaling cigarette smoke from his nostrils, he hadn't looked, but he knew it was her.

'Smoking is bad for you' Dawn replied, the first words she had spoken to him in fourteen years and she was nagging at his personal habits.

'Well, lots of things are bad for me, but it doesn't mean I don't want them', he replied

Dawn was unsure if this was a tease or if he was being serious, either way this was not a discussion they had time for now.

'You look good' she said diverting the conversation away from anything painful,

'You too' his sincerity was not as prominent.

The connection they had was severed and only time could heal it, for now they would need to be civil, they shared a common goal and that was to get Raegan back safe with her Vine. The front door flew open and another familiar face greeted her, no words were exchanged as two frail arms encased her in a long, agonising embrace, the last time they saw each other their time to say goodbye was cut short and there had been no contact exchanged since the suicide plan had been put in place all those years ago, she held Dawn tightly, squeezing the life from her lungs.

'I knew you would come back' she said pulling Dawns head over her shoulder like a baby waiting to be burped.

As she slowly released her grip Dawn could see how much time had passed, her mother was shorter now, although no weaker, her hair had thinned at the front and her skin had wrinkled around her eyes. She probably thought the same when she looked at Dawn, time had not been kind to her either, her eyes were darker around the rim and a splattering of grey hairs had risen in her once dark locks. In a flash her mother's temperament changed from joy to sadness.

'I tried to keep her safe Dawn, you have to believe me, we both did, we underestimated her abilities'

'What do you mean her abilities?' said Dawn

The eye contact between her Mother and Angelo said it all, two other bodies disturbed the moment, Dawn did not recognise the youngsters, they were only a few years younger than she was when she left,

'James, Alice, this is Dawn', said Angelo,

Dawn was stunned, not by the introduction of the two new faces but by her mother's previous statement,

'She's a mapper?' Dawn muttered under her breath ignoring the two young strangers.

The reality of the words she was speaking sinking in, how could she be? It wasn't in their Vine, most of her Vine were steerers with a few watchers but no one was a mapper. Dawn did not even know any mappers they were so rare. No wonder Raegan was of interest to Devin, he was marketing himself as the caring father when it was purely a ruse to get her on his side, he must be aware of her potential, maybe he had even coaxed it out of her to test it, nothing would surprise her.

'How do you know she's a mapper? Do you have proof?' she asked

'Unfortunately, yes' said her mother,

'There was an incident not long ago that left a man devoid'

'Devoid?' the word bounced from ear to ear, she was taken back to the snake, the incident with young Gabriel, how Raegan claimed she had told the snake to die and it had, she should have known then that something wasn't quite right, she blamed herself.

'Does she know what she is?' questioned Dawn,

'She does'.

'Is she in control of it?'

'Not exactly, but she's a got a lot of fight in her Dawn, just like you' replied her mother.

She should have been proud of her strong willed and determined daughter, but she imagined herself in Raegan's shoes, lost, out of control and lonely, not a recommended combination for a mapper.

'When did you last hear from her?' asked Dawn

'Dom was last to see her, she went to rescue him, but Devin kept her',

'Who's Dom?' said Dawn looking directly to Angelo for a response,

'I am' came a deep voice from inside the doorway,

'Skulking in the shadows, of course, a Leon, why wouldn't she fall for a Leon?' Dawn muttered under her breath.

This new face was not totally unfamiliar to her, she had seen him before, she had saved him from the Leon the night before. She had assumed as he was running from the Leon he wasn't one of them, but she was wrong. Bigger things were at play here, she could feel it, of all the people she should come across on her journey she ends up saving this Leon boy from capture and possible death. Dawn could see why Raegan would be attracted to him, like most Leon men he was alluring, his obscurity was exciting, Dawn had been beguiled in the same way.

'Where is she now Dom, where did you leave her? said Dawn impatiently,

'I didn't leave her anywhere, she stayed of her own accord, she watched them take me away',

'You must know where he would take her', said Dawn becoming exasperated by the Leon traitor.

'I wish I did' he said hanging his head in shame,

'She hasn't been close for a while; I haven't felt her' James turned to Dawn his statement sparking new hope.

'And who is this?' she said perplexed by the other attractive young male in the pack,

'Nice to meet you, I'm James, Raegan's consort', he said overly politely,

'If you were Raegan's consort you wouldn't be here' Dawn spat through her teeth dismissing him.

'Ease up Dawn, they aren't even tied yet, the kid has been doing his best, our daughter is a loose cannon, not easy to keep hold of' said Angelo

Dawn ignored his gesture, half of her angry that no one had protected her daughter and half of her proud that she had the strength to face things on her own.

'Does anyone have any idea where Raegan actually is?' Dawn asked

A silent consensus confirming her worst fear.

'Well it's a good thing have this then' she said pulling out a small wooden pendant from her pocket, Angelo smiled as all eyes peered at Dawns hand.

'You kept it' said Angelo, his voice croaky with emotion,

'Of course I did, did she?' said Dawn

'She wears it every day' he replied holding Dawns gaze,

A bond had grown between them branching their way back to being consorts. She felt warmth cocoon her body as they shared a blissful moment, Dawn had forgotten how addictive this was, how good it could make you feel. She had spent so long feeling so bad that she had given up hope of ever feeling like this again.

'This is how we find her' said Dawn

'The Vine are collected; we need to move' her Mother urged breaking the moment between the two consorts.

'The Bane are marching' said Dom staring directly at Dawn,

'It's   time'.

CHAPTER 50

RAEGAN

High school seemed such a long time ago, as Raegan walked past the tall building, she wished that her life was simple again. Where the whole world revolved around saying the right thing or wearing the right outfit, if she could go back she would try harder and be a better friend. Alice had probably given up on her by now and returned to her normal life, why wouldn't she, who would opt into all of this mess. Idle conversations between them replayed in her head, the pitiful ponderings of teenage life were a comfort. The streets were deserted with only the odd person putting out the trash or getting home from a day's work. Raegan's focus shifted to a young man carrying a briefcase from his car, obviously home from a long day at the office, well that was the story he was telling his wife. Raegan could see something quite different, a lustful montage only suitable for an adult audience, he wasn't even doing a very convincing job of hiding it. His shirt was creased down the back pleat, a brush of pink on his shoulder, the late evening return after a 'conference call'. He was greeted at the door by a woman wearing soft linen clothes with a young baby on her hip, her loose clothes hiding the blemishes of birth. The baby was content, gently sucking its fist as her father reached to relieve the tired woman. He was a cheat, his duality a flaw in this picture-perfect life. Raegan did not let his reasoning for his actions enter her mind, she just focused on the consequences. Tonight, he would confess and repair his woes, Raegan planted the seed of redemption in his mind, it was maybe the last good thing she could do with her Glimmer.

The town square was the obvious place to meet, Devin would have paid off the cops so they didn't interfere with the proceedings, and the Glimmer would have steered the rest of the town so that they wouldn't not get hurt in the crossfire. This was not about the innocent, neither side would want to draw them into it. As Raegan proceeded on her path the road beneath her began to shudder with the seismic quality of a small earthquake; the Bane were marching, their steps choreographed in perfect time. Raegan was still four blocks from the square, her walk changed to a run, her breathing besieged by her strides. Over the top of the building she could see a soft golden glow, a cloud of light expanding into the abyss, the Glimmer were projecting. Devin's main objective would be to destroy the Glimmers and convince Raegan to return to the Bane, he would not care about anyone who got in the way of his mission.

One block to go and Raegan was floored, her body slamming viciously onto the cobbled stone, an excruciating pain surging through her left side, she was paralysed. Her vision distorted in a warped fisheye lens. Feeling her way around her clothes with her right arm she searched for a wound, maybe a bullet or an arrow, something venomous must have produced this much agony, but her physical body was not damaged, she could feel someone else's pain, it was James. Shock would set in soon if she didn't gain control, Raegan clawed at the ground pushing herself back to standing, she held her left side as the shock subsided, running had become impossible as Raegan's arm flapped around of its own accord. Something else was burrowing into her, another person was trying to connect, someone she didn't know. Raegan blocked their attempts motivated by her single goal.

Turning into the square the severity of the situation hit her, so many people had gathered on both sides, it was a classic fairy-tale battle, all fighting for their heritage and a chance for their legacy to survive. This wasn't a battle with weapons, not physical ones anyway, this was more dangerous than knives and guns, it was a battle of belief. Raegan scanned the combat zone, on one side was her Vine, on the other the Bane, her gaze was drawn to a young man laying awkwardly on the ground. James lay motionless, a young woman draped over to protect him for further injury; it was Alice. Raegan's pain turned into jealously; what was going on? he was her consort not Alice's. Raegan was baffled her by her reaction, where was this resentment coming from? It ate into her psyche, burrowing deep as she looked upon the duo. Her line of sight was swiftly obstructed by other Glimmers all congregating in the square. Raegan scoured the rest of the Vine searching for her Gran, she would know what to do, she always did.

At the back of the crowd stood a lone figure shrouded in mystery, she wasn't connected in the same way the others were, she was observing the action rather than taking part. Raegan was compelled towards her, her body taking the lead leaving her mind in the chaos. Devin must have caught a glimpse of her as she moved through the crowd, the whole Bane turned their heads to face her, perfectly synchronised. Her Gran mimicked them drawing Raegan's attention straight to her.

'Raegan, you must get away, they are here to take you' she said loudly above the white noise,

'I won't need to take her anywhere Sandy, she will come with me by the end of this' Devin replied, his voice echoing above the chaos.

Raegan rushed between the two, equidistant to each.

'Don't I get a say in this? At what point do I get to decide who I am and who I want to be, this feud has gone on too long, we have a chance to bury this hatred and start again' she said, her voice carrying above her the crowd.

'It isn't that simple' said her Gran, maintaining her focus on the Leon leader.

'This feud goes back hundreds of years and we cannot let it lie; it is why we exist' insisted her Gran.

The white noise intensified, growing uncomfortable in Raegan's ears. A few of the weaker Glimmers collapsed to the side streets, some of the younger Leon's skulked off to take shelter from the pain. The strange woman at the back started to make her way to the front of the group, her strides calculated and purposeful, Raegan couldn't make out her features through the crowd, but her confidence was admirable. Devin dropped his shield, releasing the Glimmer from their agony, his face had changed, he could not mask his feelings for this stranger, she looked over to Raegan and smiled,

'You can't do this Devin; this needs to stop' Dawn said staring the Leon leader down.

He was obviously shaken by her presence. Raegan was transformed to a three-year-old, she recalled the last time he saw her mother, she remembered her listing all of her favourite things and watching her slowly ebb away into the distance as she watched from the kindergarten window, why had she never recalled any of this before? Devin still hadn't spoken a word, his eyes tracing Dawn all over to convince his brain that she was real. He must have grieved too, possibly regretted his decision over the years.

'You're alive, how are you alive? I checked everywhere, I scoured the earth for you' he said, astonishment smothering his words.

Raegan watched her mother carefully, there was no sign of remorse in her face, she was past it.

'I did what I had to do for my child, for my Vine, I sacrificed everything for them so I am not just going to let you take her away from us' said Dawn, a whip of air circling around her.

'You don't get to tell me what to do Dawn, and you don't get a say in Raegan's life, you abandoned her remember, you abandoned both of us' said Devin his face rigid with anger.

'You know it was more complicated than that, you made me do it, you forced my hand' she replied, both voices accelerating in pitch as emotions the soared.

'That's the difference between us Dawn, I would have never let anyone get in our way, I would have protected both of you if you would have given me the chance'.

Devin reignited the Bane causing a surge of power to be directed in the Glimmer direction, there were less of them now, most drained from the primary onslaught. Dawn was helpless, her Glimmer was still recovering so the full force hit her like a tornado tearing up anything in its path.

'No' Raegan screamed,

Her body pulsating with rage, she couldn't lose her again, she pounced forward her feet heavy on the concrete floor, each step sending vibrations through the earth, the ground began to crack beneath them as she moved towards her shaking Mother. She grabbed her and pulled her to the side as the crack swelled, a few of the Bane were losing their footing in the tremor and clambered to the floor clutching onto each other. Devin had not moved, his physical strength resisting the shuddering ground, his eyes wildly curious at Raegan's capabilities. Looking straight into her he pushed his palm delicately forward causing another cycle of destruction to hit. Several Glimmers were thrown from the square, Raegan searched for her Dad, he was nowhere to be seen, her visual search of the jagged landscape landed on the person that had set all of this in motion. Dom was a shadow of himself, almost unrecognisable from the boy she met a few weeks ago, his body fragile, his ego damaged. They're eyes met in the mayhem, physically there was only meters between them, but the emotional chasm continued to grow. He was in an impossible position; he couldn't desert the Bane, but he wouldn't harm the Glimmer either. Raegan didn't judge his cowardice and as he started to retreat from the conflict, she held his gaze; where this could have gone, she will never know. As he vanished into the distance Raegan felt a pang of guilt, she could add this affliction to her list.

Her patience was running thin, this needed to stop, a frenzy began to swell inside her bubbling at the bottom of her stomach, this was not nerves, it was anticipation. She wasn't sure what was going to happen, but the risk outweighed the inevitability of what was to come. Shielding her Mother from the fray Raegan imploded, flares of light shot out from her body like bullets from a gun causing time to stand still, momentum paused leaving the two crowds in limbo, the white noise reformed into mirror bubbles surrounding everyone in its wake. Fascination smeared across Devin's face as he watched

Raegan bloom, the Leon and Glimmer moulding together uniting her two innate selves into one. In the stillness he clenched his fist, a simple but destructive action. Raegan held the void for a few seconds, Leon kin were pulling away as the light became too intense, Devin could not hold them in, their biological response to flee was too strong, they were not built for this intensity. Raegan became aware of the impact it was having, her Glimmer kin were falling too, weary from strength she had taken from them. She gently released the Glimmer and like many of the crown including Devin, she collapsed, all energy sapped leaving her a shell on the ground.

Raegan was not sure if she was fully conscious, her eyes were looking up at the star spattered sky, but her head was not processing it. Sound echoed between her ears causing chaos in her mind as she regained the feeling in her body. Her skin felt the pain first as burning coated it, thousands of pin pricks simultaneously piercing through, she couldn't scream, this had to be done in silence. Enduring the agony was the price that had to be paid for projecting her Glimmer. As she tuned back into the world Raegan could hear only cries, lots of harrowing cries. Her mother was lying beside her but she was not moving, Raegan fumbled on her neck to check for a pulse, she was still alive, she looked around frantically for the others, her Dad was stirring on the ground, Alice was tending to James who was still in agony from his first injury. She couldn't see her Gran, she had been standing directly behind them, her flow had been feeding directly into the Raegan's, she scoured the ground moving desperately through the dazed bodies moving from person to person to check for a response; no fatalities, she breathed a sigh of release, her Vine were safe.

Sweat and grime dripped from her forehead as she rested in a heap on the ground, the Leon had retreated from the square leaving just a few wounded to make their own way back. Devin was nowhere to be seen, missing in the devastation, Raegan shouldn't have cared after what he had done to her Vine, but she did care. Returning to her feet she roamed to the outskirts of the crowd, the harrowing effects of the feud becoming real, she reached a frail body on the outskirts of the group, this body wasn't moving and it was contorted uncomfortably with thick red liquid trickling from its head. Raegan didn't need to approach the body to know who it was, she knew, they all knew. Her Mother approached her from behind, their reunion cut short by the tragedy laid in front of them. Confused in the chaos her Mother flinched as she realised who was lying on the ground, a deep and guttural sob left her mouth as she hurdled towards the body, a mass of others crowded around intrigued by the unsettling sounds. Raegan stepped back out of the crowd, continuing back until she came to a halt.

'You did this you know; this wasn't me' said Devin, an awe of pride engraved in his words.

'Your powers are too strong for you, you can't control them safety' he continued, his allegiance open and obvious to Raegan.

She began to sob, her throat filling with guilt.

'I didn't mean to' she said, her words turning into her own blubbered dialect.

'You know what you have to do', he continued.

Yes, she knew, and she knew he had foreseen this, and he knew what she would choose.

'You need to do this for the safety of your Vine Raegan, you don't want any more of them to fall foul of your glitch, come with me and I will help you perfect your abilities'

Glitch, that was a good word for Raegan, she was a glitch, her power was not wanted, she was an unnatural glitch in the system, a biproduct of youthful stupidity. She was going into shock, her tears painting a blank expression on her face, her body moving robotically,   what   had   she   done?

CHAPTER 51

DAWN

The void had only lasted a few seconds in real time but had felt like forever whilst inside it, she couldn't comprehend what had happened, the void itself would not have killed her mother, she was stronger than that, something else must have occurred during it. Her body had gone into automatic grief; she couldn't remember much happening but her own wailing still rang clearly in her ears. She was now in shock, curled up like a foetus on the pavement, hugging her knees closely into her chest for comfort. In all of the madness she had forgotten about Raegan, she had resigned herself to not thinking about her whilst she was in exile because the pain was too much to handle, but now she needed to step up to be the parent she knew she could be. Unfolding herself she scoured the human debris for Raegan,

'Alice, have you seen Raegan?' she said walking delicately through the mashup of Glimmers scattered on the sidewalk.

Alice shook her head, her mind muted by the tragedy of the events. Dawn continued to make her way through the Vine questioning each person about the whereabouts of her daughter, then she came to James, sitting in distress and pain, Dawn bent down to soothe him.

'James, it's me, Dawn' she said softly, his eyelids were charred with soot and the left side of his body limp.

'James, have you seen Raegan?', he couldn't look back at her, his eyes wondered of their own accord trying to focus,

'I can't see anything' he sobbed, the realisation of his future striking Dawn,

'But I know where she is, I can see her with him in my head, he knew this would happen, he planned it to happen, this was the way to get her to go with him'.

Dawn clasped the pendant around her neck, is wooden shine reduced to scorched ash. Dawns breath turned shallow, she knew he had orchestrated this, he had orchestrated it all, her return, Raegan's void, he had killed her Mother and now he has her daughter, this wasn't about them, this was about Dawn; this was payback.

Dawn rose to standing looking out to the dark side of town, a party had begun in celebration of their feat, laser lights and lanterns filled the skies, a welcome home for the daughter of Devin, the princess. To get her back she would need to be smarter and stronger than them all and she wouldn't give up this time, not ever.

CHAPTER 52

RAEGAN

3 months later...

Her new life brought challenges; she couldn't deny that. Her world was different to before, sure she missed her Vine, her friends and him but this was the best thing for all of them. They were safe from harm. Raegan had renounced her Glimmer so she could no longer feel James' pain, but it had taken a few weeks to fade. His blackness was her blackness; his fear was her fear. It had to stop. Alice would take care of him, she was sure of that, Her Mother hadn't initiated contact, but Raegan wasn't surprised, she was responsible for her Grans death and it was something she could never be repaid. From what she had found out, her Dad was an empty shell, his world buried in woe from the loss of Raegan. Devin had consoled her to begin with but soon became tired of her grief, so now she hid it, bottled it up so tight that it became invisible. A time capsule of sorrow that one day would be unearthed by an unlucky soul. She was not sure what the future would bring but something rooted deep inside her told knew that this was not the end. Bigger things awaited her, and the Leon princess would one day be the Leon queen.

Printed in Poland
by Amazon Fulfillment
Poland Sp. z o.o., Wrocław

58821300R00183